AFTER THE LOST WAR

By Andrew Hudgins

Saints and Strangers
After the Lost War

AFTER THE LOST WAR

A NARRATIVE

ANDREW HUDGINS

HOUGHTON MIFFLIN COMPANY
BOSTON
1988

Library of Congress Cataloging-in-Publication Data

Hudgins, Andrew.
After the lost war.
I. Title.
PS3558.U288A69 1988 811'.54 87-16963
ISBN 0-395-45712-2
ISBN 0-395-45713-0 (pbk.)

Printed in the United States of America

Q 10 9 8 7 6 5 4 3 2 1

For Randall Curb, Tom Doherty, Nancy Loeb,
John Reese — *sustaining friends*

What wretched errors hath my heart committed
Whilst it hath thought itself so blessed never!
How have mine eyes out of their spheres been fitted,
In the distraction of this madding fever!
O benefit of ill! Now I find true
That better is by evil still made better.

Shakespeare, Sonnet CXIX

History repeats itself. That's one of the things that's wrong with history.

Clarence Darrow

CONTENTS

PREFACE

This sequence of poems is based on the life of the Georgia-born poet and musician Sidney Lanier. Though the poems are all spoken by a character I call Sidney Lanier, the voice of these poems will be unfamiliar to anyone who knows the writings of this historical figure. Despite his having been dead for over a hundred years now, I'd like to thank Lanier for allowing me to use the facts of his life — more or less — to see how I might have lived it if it had been mine. And, in too many ways, I suppose it has.

I

THE MACON VOLUNTEERS

Sidney Lanier was born in Macon, Georgia, in 1842. At nineteen, after graduating from Oglethorpe College, he joined the Macon Volunteers and was sent to Virginia, where he fought in the battle of Chancellorsville and in various smaller skirmishes. Later, he, along with his beloved brother Clifford, was transferred to the Signal Corps; and still later, in 1864, he was assigned to the ship *Lucy*. While attempting to run the federal blockade off the coast of Wilmington, North Carolina, the *Lucy* was captured and Lanier taken prisoner. He was transported to Fort Lookout, Maryland, where he was confined for three months under extremely brutal conditions. As a result, Lanier's health, never very strong, broke completely, and he remained, with ups and downs, a semi-invalid for the rest of his life.

Released from prison at war's end, he staggered, half alive, through the Carolinas, home to Macon.

In 1867 Lanier proposed marriage to Virginia Hankins and was rejected. Almost immediately he proposed to Mary Day, the daughter of a Macon jeweler, and was accepted. In the spring of 1863, on leave from his regiment, he had met Mary at the home of a mutual friend, where they had played duets, he on the flute, she on the piano.

CHILD ON THE MARSH

I worked the river's slick banks, grabbling
in mud holes underneath tree roots.
You'd think it would be dangerous,
but I never came up with a cooter
or cottonmouth hung on my fingertips.
Occasionally, though, I leapt upright,
my fingers hooked through the red gills
of a mudcat. And then I thrilled
the thrill my father felt when he
burst home from fishing, drunk, and yelled,
well before dawn, *"Wake up! Come here!"*
He tossed some fatwood on the fire
and flames raged, spat, and flickered. He held
a four-foot mudcat. *"I caught it!"*
he yelled. *"I caught this monster!"* At first,
dream-dazed, I thought it was something
he'd saved us from. By firelight, the fish
gleamed wickedly. But Father laughed
and hugged me hard, pressing my head
against his coat, which stank, and glittered
where dried scales caught the light. For breakfast,
he fried enormous chunks of fish,
the whole house glorious for days
with their rich stink. One scale stuck to my face,
and as we ate he blinked, until
he understood what made me glitter.
He laughed, reached over, flicked the star
off of my face. That's how I felt
— that wild! — when I jerked struggling fish
out of the mud and held them up,
long muscles shuddering on my fingers.

Once, grabbling, I got lost. I traced
the river to the marsh, absorbed
with fishing, then absorbed with ants.
With a flat piece of bark, I'd scoop
red ants onto a black-ant hill
and watch. Then I would shovel black
ants on a red-ant hill to see
what difference that would make.
Not much. And I returned to grabbling,
then skimming stones. Before I knew it,
I'd worked my way from fresh water to salt,
and I was lost. Sawgrass waved, swayed,
and swung above my head. Pushed down,
it sprang back. Slashed at, it slashed back.
All I could see was sawgrass. Where was
the sea, where land? With every step,
the mud sucked at my feet with gasps
and sobs that came so close to speech
I sang in harmony with them.
My footprints filled with brine as I
walked on, still fascinated with
the sweat bees, hornets, burrow bees;
and, God forgive me, I was not afraid
of anything. Lost in sawgrass,
I knew for sure just *up* and *down*.
Almost enough. Since then, they are
the only things I've had much faith in.
Night fell. The slow moon rose from sawgrass.
Soon afterward I heard some cries
and answered them. So I was saved
from things I didn't want to be

saved from. Ma tested her green switch
— *zip! zip!* — then laid it on my thighs,
oh, maybe twice, before she fell,
in tears, across my neck. She sobbed
and combed my hair of cockleburs.
She laughed as she dabbed alcohol
into my cuts. I flinched. She chuckled.
And even as a child, I heard,
inside her sobs and chuckling,
the lovely sucking sound of earth
that followed me, gasped, called my name
as I stomped through the mud, wrenched free,
and heard the earth's voice under me.

AT CHANCELLORSVILLE

THE BATTLE OF THE WILDERNESS

He was an Indiana corporal
shot in the thigh when their line broke
in animal disarray. He'd crawled
into the shade and bled to death.
My uniform was shabby with
continuous wear, worn down to threads
by the inside friction of my flesh on cloth.
The armpit seams were rotted through
and almost half the buttons had dropped off.
My brother said I should remove
the Yank's clean shirt: "From now on, Sid,
he'll have no use for it." Imagining
the slack flesh shifting underneath
my hands, the other-person stink
of that man's shirt, so newly his,
I cursed Clifford from his eyeballs to
his feet. I'd never talked that way before
and didn't know I could. When we returned,
someone had beat me to the shirt.
So I had compromised my soul
for nothing I would want to use —
some knowledge I could do without.
Clifford, thank God, just laughed. It was good
stout wool, unmarked by blood.
By autumn, we wore so much blue
we could have passed for New York infantry.

AFTER THE WILDERNESS

MAY 3, 1863

When Clifford wasn't back to camp by nine,
I went to look among the fields of dead
before we lost him to a common grave.
But I kept tripping over living men
and had to stop and carry them to help
or carry them until they died,
which happened more than once upon my back.
And I got angry with those men because
they kept me from my search and I was out
still stumbling through the churned-up earth at dawn,
stopping to stare into each corpse's face,
and all the while I was writing in my head
the letter I would have to send our father,
saying Clifford was lost and I had lost him.

I found him bent above a dying squirrel
while trying to revive the little thing.
A battlefield is full of trash like that —
dead birds and squirrels, bits of uniform.
Its belly racked for air. It couldn't live.
Cliff knew it couldn't live without a jaw.
When in relief I called his name, he stared,
jumped back, and hissed at me like a startled cat.
I edged up slowly, murmuring "Clifford, Cliff,"
as you might talk to calm a skittery mare,
and then I helped him kill and bury all
the wounded squirrels he'd gathered from the field.
It seemed a game we might have played as boys.
We didn't bury them all at once, with lime,
the way they do on burial detail,
but scooped a dozen, tiny, separate graves.

When we were done he fell across the graves
and sobbed as though they'd been his unborn sons.
His chest was large — it covered most of them.
I wiped his tears and stroked his matted hair,
and as I hugged him to my chest I saw
he'd wet his pants. We called it Yankee tea.

ON THE KILLING FLOOR

The cows moaned deep bass lows that rumbled in
their bellies as I toddled under them,
a child of four. I'd crawled beneath the fence
to feel the huge notes tremble on my flesh.
My short head scraping on their bellies, I walked

between tall legs, feet gumming in the mud
of the small pen outside the slaughterhouse.
I've marveled at how placidly they go
to death, as, later still, I marveled at
how cheerfully in war men march to death

and me in step with them. A penned-up herd
of horses might have spooked and trampled me.
But cows are stupid meat. How large they were!
Great docile things that somehow frightened me
by size alone. What else about a cow

is there to frighten anyone, except
how well behaved they are in line to die?
If you stare most beasts in the eye — dogs, cats —
you see a fleck of light that might be called
a soul. In cows' thick, clouded, mud-colored eyes,

I've never seen a thing. Is that light why
we don't eat horses, dogs, or cats
unless we must? Horse isn't bad. But that
is all I know about forbidden flesh.
And which was I among those moaning cows?

They jostled slowly one against the other.
I grabbed a heifer's tail and followed her

onto the killing floor. I don't recall
the nine-pound hammer's soft report, the cow's
thud as she fell, the sudden twisting of

her tail, which I would not let go, my gasp
as a huge black man swung me by the waist
and said, "Don't rush. You'll get here soon enough."
He laughed and carried me beneath his arm
to Mama, who says she screamed and wept.

I don't remember any of these things.
But I'll remember till I die the way
she switched me with a green althea switch
I had to choose myself. *Swick, swick,* it said
across my butt. *Don't be so curious.*

SERENADES IN VIRGINIA

SUMMER 1863

1.

When we heard of a lady who
was said to be a stunning beauty,
we went to serenade her charms.
We were denied by summer rain —
a gully washer that got in my flute
before I played a single bar.
With Clifford's extra guitar string,
we tied a note to her doorknob, and left.

Next week, we were invited back
for meals that made the table bow:
Virginia ham, stuffed eggs, roast hens,
and mounds of biscuits I sopped full
of honey then ate with a spoon
when they collapsed. Our gracious hosts
insisted that we spend the night.
We did. A pleasant yellow slave
brought us mint juleps as we rose.

2.

To stop our signal flags, the Yanks
sent several hundred men. But we
smelled out their trap and answered it
with such firepower they did not,
thank God, perceive we numbered less
than twenty men. Across two miles
of sumac and a second growth of pine,
which we relinquished inch by inch,
we poured great quantities of lead
into their ranks and watched their lines
collapse. It seemed almost a lark.

But I see clear in memory
what I ignored back then: the dull
inhuman thud of lead on flesh,
the buckling of a shot man's knees,
the outward fling of arms, and the
short arc a head inscribes before
it hits the ground. The war, my God,
had been over for two long years
before I understood that they,
the Yanks we killed, were human too.

3.

To His Father

But in the rush and scrabble of the raid
we lost *Aurora Leigh, Les Misérables,*
volumes of Shelley, Coleridge, and Keats,
and one by Heine. Secure at any price
the works of Uhland, Schelling, Tieck.
Because my flute was in my haversack,
it wasn't lost. I'm well. Don't fear for me.

4.

Miss Hankins was a handsome girl.
Not pretty — handsome. Her forehead was
too broad, her lips too thin, for pretty.
But she was full of life, possessed
a mind that almost rivaled mine,
and had a solemn faith — in me.
One night as we sat in the swing,
I made, for her, a rendering
of Heine's "Du bist wie eine Blume."

And when it landed on my hand
I brushed a firefly off and said,
"Fly thou away and know that once
in midst of summer greenness thou
didst light upon a poet's hand."
And Ginna Hankins never cracked a smile.
A girl like that's beyond compare —
a pearl! a ruby! After the war
I asked her to become my wife.
She said she couldn't leave her brothers
without a woman in the house.
Within a month I was engaged
to Mary Day. I couldn't wait.
To this day we still correspond.

5.

To W. A. Hopson

I should have answered long ago.
But I've indulged myself so thoroughly
in chills and fever, I've had scant time
for food and drink. Or correspondence.

Miss H. is here. She presses me
to send her warmest sentiments
and say she's humbly satisfied
that your one friend in Franklin of her sex
is cross-eyed, dull, and otherwise
devoid of grace, because, she adds,
you'll have less call to tarry there.
It's true. Speed back. We need your bass
to add a bottom to our sing-alongs.

6.

When Cliff and I discuss the war,
we talk of lovely women, serenades,
the moonlit dashes on the beach,
the brushes of our force with theirs,
with whom we clashed with more élan
and consequence. We had enough
hair's-breadth escapes to keep our spirits high.
What a godforsaken war it would have been
if we'd run short of decent horses!

But there are many things we don't recall.
Like Hopson, who, at Gettysburg,
had one heel sliced off by a minié ball.
He sings as deeply as he ever did
but does it leaning slightly to the left.

AROUND THE CAMPFIRE

Around the campfire we sang hymns.
When asked, I'd play my flute and lay
a melody between night's
incessant cannonfire, which boomed
irregularly but with the depth
of kettle drums. Occasionally,
in lulls, we'd hear a fading snatch
of Yankee song sucked to us in
the backwash of their cannonballs.
These are, oddly enough, fond memories.

One night, a Texas boy sat down
and strummed a homemade banjo.
He'd bought it for a canteen full
of corn. He followed me around
and pestered me to teach him notes.
He loved that ragged box but, Lord,
he couldn't play it worth a damn.
Nobody could. I tried to tell him so.
"Hell, I know, Sid," he said. "If I
were any good, it would worry me
too much. This way I can just blame
the instrument."

And this, too, is
a fond instructive memory.

Boom BOOM. "Listen to *that*," he said.
Then silence once again as Yanks
swabbed out the cannon barrel and rammed
another charge into the gun. They paused
a minute in their work. *Boom BOOM*.

Our cannon fired in answer to
incoming shells. “Don’t they,” he asked,
“sound like a giant limping through
the woods in search of us?” I laughed.
It was a peaceful night and we
were working on some liquid corn.
Boom BOOM. I filled my cup again
and said, “He’s after us, all right.”
He laughed. *Boom BOOM*. I sloshed more in
his cup. A shell exploded to our right.
A piece of shrapnel nicked my ear,
and when the smoke had cleared, I saw
him sitting, looking for his cup
and for the hand he’d held it in.

From this, I didn’t learn a thing.

THE HORNETS' NEST

We may have been just nine or ten, but still
we knew it was a stupid thing to do.
The drone drew us. We found it hanging, plump,
beneath a cypress limb, vibrant with risk
and fat with danger. That's what drew us, that's

what made us hit it with a rotten limb
I found nearby. Though we weren't ten years old,
we felt, as boys, the dumb destructive need
to show we had some power in the world.
Not much. But some. The swinging broke the stick,

but one piece hit the nest, pierced it. When wasps
exploded from the wound, we were already running
beneath the frightening verticality of moss
that hung, like beards, from ancient cypresses.
We ran toward water. We'd thought that far ahead.

Two splashes. Joab made it. So did I.
Jack tripped. They settled on him like a ghost.
He blurred beneath the frenzy of their wings.
"Get up!" we hollered from the water. *"Run!"*
He rose, and staggered to the marsh. They clung

around him like a nimbus as he lurched
toward us. *"Come on, come on!"* we yelled, then ducked
beneath the water as the wasps arrived.
They circled, swooped each time we stuck our heads
up for a breath of air. Once I was safe

I lay back in the warm mud and enjoyed
stealing my breath. The danger made it fun

to jab my face back into the surface world,
suck in some air and sink contentedly
into the marsh. Jack's eyes had swollen shut,

and oozed. We led him home and told his ma
it was an accident. Eight years or nine.
I did the proper things. I visited.
I wrote. But what I thought was this: *I'm glad*
it's him. I'm glad it's not me. Eight years old.

BURIAL DETAIL

Between each layer of tattered, broken flesh
we spread, like frosting, a layer of lime,
and then we spread it extra thick on top
as though we were building a giant torte.
The lime has something to do with cholera
and helps, I think, the chemistry of decay
when slathered between the ranks of sour dead.
I know what we did; I'm not sure why.
The colonel had to ask us twice for volunteers;
the second time, I went. I don't know why.
Even in August heat I cannot sleep
unless I have a sheet across my shoulders.
I guess we owe our species something.
We stacked the flaccid meat all afternoon,
and then night fell so black and absolute
it was as if the day had never been,
was something impossible we'd made up
to comfort ourselves in our long work.
And even in the pitch-black, pointless dark
we stacked the men and spread the lime
as we had done all day. Though not as neat.

They were supposed to be checked thoroughly.
I didn't look; I didn't sift their pockets.
A lot of things got buried that shouldn't have.
I tossed men unexamined into the trench.
But out of the corners of my eyes
I kept seeing faces I thought I knew.
At first they were faces of anonymous men
I may have seen in camp or on the field.
Later, as I grew tired, exhausted, sick,

I saw they were my mother, father, kin
whom I had never seen but recognized
by features I knew in different combinations
on the shifting, similar faces of my cousins,
and even, once, a face that looked like mine.
But when I stopped to stare at them
I found the soft, unfocused eyes of strangers,
and let them drop into the common grave.

Then, my knees gave. I dropped my shovel
and pitched, face first, into the half-filled trench.
I woke almost immediately, and stood
on someone's chest while tired hands pulled me out.
It's funny — standing there, I didn't feel
the mud-wet suck of death beneath my feet
as I had felt it often enough before
when we made forced marches through Virginia rain.
That is to say, the dead man's spongy chest
was firmer than the roads that led us —
and him — into the Wilderness.
For six or seven days I had to hear
a lot of stupid jokes about that faint:
Folks are dying to get in — that sort of thing.
I wasn't the only one to faint.
You would think I would have fainted for my father,
for some especially mutilated boy,
for Clifford or my mother. Not for myself.

In the hot, inexhaustible work of the night
a good wind blowing from a distant storm
was heaven, more so because the bodies needed

to be wet, to ripen in moisture and lime,
to pitch and rock with tiny lives,
or whatever it takes to make them earth again.
Okay, I'm sorry for this, for getting worked up.
The thought that they might not decay
was enough to make my stomach heave.
Some men I've argued with seem to think
that they'll stay perfect, whole and sweet,
beneath the ground. It makes me shudder:
dead bodies in no way different from my own
except mine moves, and shudders in its moving.
I take great comfort in knowing I will rot
and that the chest I once stood on
is indistinguishable from other soil
and I will be indistinguishable from it.

But standing there, looking out of the grave,
eyes barely above the lip of earth, I saw
the most beautiful thing I've ever seen:
dawn on the field after the Wilderness.
The bodies, in dawn light, were simply forms;
the landscape seemed abstract, unreal.
It didn't look like corpses, trees, or sky,
but shapes on shapes against a field of gray.
In short, it looked like nothing human.
But the sun broke from the horizon soon enough
and we could see exactly what we'd done.

A SOLDIER ON THE MARSH

On leave, I sat on marsh grass, watched
bees tremble into new red blooms,
and thought of how, a boy, I'd put
my finger on the backs of bees.
Engrossed, they didn't notice me,
and I, careful, wouldn't touch them long,
a second or two, but long enough
to feel the hard hum of their wings.
I never got stung. Clifford did.
And Mother whipped me with a belt
for showing him my trick. He asked.
She was more dangerous than bees,
and danger was what fascinated me
so much I'd wait until a bee
crawled in a morning glory bloom.
I'd pinch the flower shut and shake
the bloom, loving the angry buzz,
the danger I had trapped. The war
has killed that stupid fascination —
"D-E-D, dead," as Father says.

Blue as blood hidden in the body,
storm winds tore at oak leaves, which raged
like green birds limed to whipping limbs.
Dead limbs dislodged. Pine cones and acorns
swept toward me as I shut my eyes,
lay underneath an oak, and listened.
They sounded like a giant's feet
approaching, blundering from the west.
A thick branch skittered through the limbs
and hit six inches from my head.

I lay there through the storm, got drenched,
took off my clothes, and draped them on
a redbud tree. As they dried, I,
nude, played my flute. I caught
the trills and cadence of the birds
and was rewarded when a far
wood thrush responded to my music,
not note for note, not harmony,
but just enough to let me know
I'd swayed, a little bit, her song.

As I reached for my clothes, sunset
— red as blood liberated from the body —
fell over me, and, from the redbud tree,
a clumsy panicked bird, a cardinal,
exploded. One wingtip brushed my chest
an inch below the nipple, and,
in that red light off blood-red things
— blooms, bird — my whole white body turned
to flame, an *ignis fatuus,*
will-o'-the-wisp, a brief, bright light
that flickers on the marsh and means
delusion, which is my greatest gift.

Near home, the fields were bright with fire.
A farmer burning off his land
had walked the border of the marsh,
plunging a torch into the underbrush.
But where a dozen fires converged
I found a bright green tulip tree.
Leaves quivered in the winds that whipped

across the closing fires, then flared,
like torches, one by one, before
flames even touched them. Inside
the green wood, hot sap chortled, sang,
until the branches blew apart
like overheated cannon. The tree
was opening itself to fire.
I watched. I stood and watched as it
was blasted in the burning air.
The trunk collapsed, broke into embers.
Their tiny lights sprawled constellations
across the smoldering black earth.
As they consumed themselves, went dark,
the true stars came out, one beyond the next,
and in redbuds beyond burnt ground
a bobwhite sang its stupid, cheerful name.

THE LAST TIME I SAW GENERAL LEE

AN IDYLL

After we'd sung a song, the general
appeared with his camp chair. The services
began. That terrible battery, Number Two,
was firing very slowly, each crash making

the otherwise silence more silent yet,
and calm. Even Hoke's line had fallen quiet.
I hunkered by an oak and stared at him.
He was fatigued by loss of sleep. All night

incoming shells exploded near our tents.
We were under siege — at Petersburg —
and beans were scarce. But as the preacher spoke,
the spring influence of the sun relaxed

the general's face. Because no muscle moved
and he sat ramrod straight, his forearms crossed,
I wouldn't swear he slept, except I saw
a fly crawl unobstructed on his brow

and down his cheek. As large and pleasing words
fell from the preacher's lips, as lazy guns
hurled shells within two hundred yards of us,
as, finally, a mockingbird lit on

a branch above my head and piped a song
between the roar of war machinery,
it seemed to me as if the present earth
had floated off. The antique world returned,

and some majestic god dozed in our midst,
presiding at a clash of human passion,
both terrifying and sublime. And like
an ancient god, he could assist our cause,

but couldn't save us from our fate.

WAR'S END

1. At Home

Birds trilled as if it were their last
day on earth — massed, hysterical,
as if they had to reach a pitch
the other side of sound before
they left the back yard oak. I dreamt
of horses pissing near my head.
In Signal Corps, we learned to sleep
with our mouths closed. I couldn't get
into my fevered head the fact
that I was home. My dreams lagged back,
still visioning the war, like men
who straggle home reluctantly
from defeat. I believed the birds
would never hit the pitch required
to let them fly back North. I don't
even know what they were. Crows? Jays?
Or sparrows? Each time my fever broke
birds still were gathering, and growing
louder with each arrival. At first
I thought I somehow caused the racket.
But Father told me what it was.
Then I'd slip back into the fever,
wake up, and have to be set straight
all over. I lay in bed three months,
drifting from fever to the raw,
harsh world that waited for me when
the fever eased. When I got home,
Mother took to her bed. She lived
through two contented afternoons,
then died. If I had stayed away,
she would have lived forever, waiting.

I drifted into fever, woke
asking for her, was told she'd died,
and had to grieve again. That spring
she died, to me, three times.
At ten, I played beneath the house
while Mother looked for me. I played
until a red wasp stung my arm,
then I ran shouting, *"Mama, Mama."*
Angry, she wrenched my arm straight out
and rummaged in a kitchen drawer.
She found a tin of snuff, worked some
inside her mouth, then slapped the wad
across the sting. I don't recall
the sting. The cure I can't forget.
She held me twisting by the wrist
until it dried: half punishment,
half cure. I dreamed of that. One night
I dreamed I saw my future wife.
But in the dream she had green eyes.
Perhaps it means nothing. But fever
plays games. In a poem, I called myself
Death's Wife. I meant Death's Husband. Now
I wonder what insight I almost had.
Three bitter months I cuddled hard
with Death. It was our honeymoon.
Who knows if I was bride or groom?
When I got well enough and when
the birds at last had flown, I stood
and watched our neighbor paint his house.
Four times. It was that sort of spring.
Slowly the house grew brighter till

he painted it fierce yellow like
a house out of a fairy tale.
He drank, painted, and drank. By noon
he was blind drunk, painting out past
the corners of the bright house, slapping
trees, bushes, and even, once, his dog —
a one-eared hound without a name,
which, preferring to stay black,
grew wary and kept out of reach.
In August light, the yellow house
shone like a bonfire in the sun,
like light on light. For us, it was
a terrible, bitter peace. And while
the whole world as we knew it fell,
the sky turned blue, trees turned the shade
of green I dreamt about as eyes.
All changed, so thoroughly oblivious
to war, defeat, and suffering
I heard it whispering the words
that whipped my weak flesh: *Life goes on.*
And in my dreams I marched.

2. Confusion Boats

The hard part was a piece of cake.

At night, the English captain steered
the *Lucy* through the ships that blocked
our coast. By sheer chance, after we
had made the sanctuary of the gulf,
a federal cruiser spotted us
and fired a shot that shrieked

across our bow. A fine shot. We
hove to, and sat. While English sailors pulled
their sloppy uniforms in shape,
I divvied up the currency
among the men. I overlooked,
it seems, one tough old salt who worked
bare-chested in the hold. Claws out,
a tattooed blue cat clambered over
his shoulder, chasing a blue mouse
that was six inches from — I'm told —
dark sanctuary in his ass.
Frozen, the mouse could not escape.
The cat could never catch the mouse —
one trapped in mad pursuit and one
in wilder ecstasy of escape.
I gave the man my share, except
a twenty-dollar gold piece that
I hid so deeply in my flesh
it wasn't found. A golden mouse.
I could have dressed in British whites
but I disdained. The damn war stretched
from *Ivanhoe* to *Old Mortality*.
And when the Yankees trundled me
aboard the *Santiago de Cuba*
I thought, *Although I love Wordsworth,*
it is a more poetic name
than Lucy. I noticed such things.

I tucked the flute inside my sleeve
and sailed, stiff armed, to prison camp.

3. Buzzards

The buzzards hung astride the air
above the silence of Cold Harbor,

their pale unfeathered heads smeared bright
with gore. Not just the blood of horses —

the blood of men I'd marched beside.
Or men I'd fought against and helped

convert into such lumps of flesh.
I wasn't at Cold Harbor, but

I heard of it from those who were —
caged men with little else to do

but talk. In prison we had time
to study buzzards. Aloft, intent,

they questioned us, inquired about
our health — more interested than friends

who nod, asking, "How are you today?"
Though dying, we wouldn't let them land.

Even the Yankee guards abhorred
the birds. They fired at them and cursed.

The buzzards glided back, up high
and out of rifleshot, attracted by

our pre-death stink — to them as sweet
as nectar to a hummingbird.

4. The Double Rainbow

When it was not against my lips,
I tucked the flute inside my sleeve
and held the left arm motionless
and stiff. At night, since fires were banned,
we huddled in the cold and passed
our few worn, outlawed instruments
so everyone would have a chance
to disappear, like notes, inside
the larger surge of song — our most
reliable escape. But once
I lost a happy afternoon
watching the dark, taut cavalry pants
of a dying man. On them, there clung,
like fine, close-stitched embroidery,
the purple thistles of the battlefield
his horse had dragged him through. Because
they glittered vividly on coarse
blue wool, I would not pick them off.
Bright blooms and sharp-edged randomness
pinned to the flesh beneath the cloth
enchanted me. Things regular
had lost whatever grace they once
possessed. A flaw. On clear nights, stars
opened one light behind the next
to comfort us, sometimes, with their
irrational geometry,
and when the soldier died, the seeds
were buried with his flesh, as stars,
on cloud-swept nights, are buried in the sky.
But I lived on to see, amid

diarrhea, dysentery, itch,
and fever, a double rainbow bridge
the eastern sky — from nowhere to
nowhere. They awed me most because
they didn't mean a thing: it rained,
it stopped, the double rainbow shone
for just a quarter hour. The world,
God says, will never end in flood.
Who gives a good damn *how* it ends?
A soldier has small preference
if he is killed by bayonet
or minié ball. God's promise: death.
Except a man I met in prison
said he had turned in panic, run,
then staggered like a drunk. Although
his knees went slack, he didn't fall.
He saw the bayonet jut from his chest,
angled before his eyes. The blade
withdrew. He fell down on his face
and lived. He didn't die. He said
it was the most religious thing
he'd ever seen. God's promise: life.
The rainbow's heart was everything
it arched — from nowhere to nowhere,
the somehow good, the somehow beautiful.

5. In the Hold

After four months of prison camp,
I loved the hold. Is it, in dark,
you have no body, or — reversed —
in dark, body is all you have?

With my gold coin I'd bribed my name
onto the exchange list. But on the ship
it was so cold that hard, dazed men huddled
together, wrapped around each other —
that unconcerned about the way
we warmed ourselves. We hugged the pile
and tried to find enough fire there
to stay alive. I would have died
except a stronger man played flute,
poorly. A passenger, a girl, called down
to say she liked the tune. "Thanks, ma'am,"
he said, "but I can't play for shucks.
You ought to hear this other guy.
You won't though. I'm afeared Sid's dying."

"Sid who? What is his name?" It was
Ella, whom I had taught the scales
when she was twelve. Sheer chance. Men passed
my almost-corpse above their heads,
then Yankee sailors pulled me up on deck.
I'd been unconscious for two days.
I woke in Ella's berth. I woke
screaming. The warmth that saved my life
convulsed me like ten-penny nails
as it pulsed through my hands and feet,
pinning reluctant soul to slack,
distrusted flesh — just when the soul
thought it had slipped away. Hot soup
and brandy. Heat. Delirium.
And that damn girl who saved my life.
I wonder what tune Ella heard.

What song saved my life? The second day,
near midnight, I asked for my flute
and played an easy piece — some Strauss.
Below me in the hold, my friends
blasted a cheer up through the wood.
I felt it in my feet. Because,
against the odds, by sheerest, blind,
dumb-bastard chance, I wasn't dead,
they cheered for me. They cheered and cheered.

Ashore, I waved to Ella, turned,
put one raw foot before the other,
and started back to Georgia — home! —
as if the sunlight were flesh and I
a ghost who walked through its hot body.

6. The Road Home

My boots stayed damp with suppuration,
sweat, blood, body ooze. But what
began in soggy steps moved on
to something much like grace, as if
my will, floating six feet off the earth,
dragged my worn body after it
as a kite will drag a tail of rags
into the air. I can't recall
the order of events. They happened but
they really didn't, since I don't
remember when. Like dreams, but dreams
you can't dismiss as simply dreams.
These are my actual life: Once, hungry,
I left the road to beg for food.

As I approached the door, a small dog
exploded from an open window,
jumped on a nearby shed, then pulled
himself, barely, onto the roof
and howled. Because I wore my old
slouch hat and thin hair swept my neck,
the lady let him bark. I yelled
to be heard over him, asking for food.
While I stood in the yard and chewed
a yellow slab of cornbread,
he never once let up. I said,
"Thank you." She nodded once. The dog
raced back and forth along the roof,
yapping. I would have paid in gold
for that damn dog — to strangle it —
but no more coins popped from my flesh.
The moment my foot touched the road,
she said, "Hush, Boots," and then, at last,
the goddamn dog shut up. I loathed
Boots more than any soldier whom
I killed. I even knew his name,
which helps. Before or after that,
a farmer I met on the road
shared with me half a pan of pork
so rank it smelled like frying sweat.
I knelt to wash my mouth and saw,
wrinkling their fluted edges in
the white reflection of my face,
leeches. I reached into the pond
to pluck them from my face. They seized
my hand. I hadn't thought there was

enough blood left inside my skin
to lure a leech, the veal-white heart
bent backward on itself by all
the death it takes to stay alive.
I bit four leeches from my hand
and spat them in the pond. Amused,
the farmer said, "Them leeches are
a nasty piece of work." I laughed,
but the sharp taste of blood flushed out
the bad meat that had fouled my mouth
with rot.

Another time, I'm sure
a red fox trotted, tippy-toed, by me.
His black paws made him seem to float
above the red dirt road. *Human,* he said,
there's danger on the road through here.

"Ah, Fox," I said, "you have acquired
a reputation as a sweet
deceiver."

He grinned. *I know. I know.*
But there is nothing I can gain
from you, Human.

"Nothing that I can see."
His sharp head twisting up at me,
he grinned. *I like the way you think,*
he said. He led me down a path
he claimed was safer than the road.
When our trail joined the road again
I offered him a piece of pork
the farmer had given me.

It stinks,
the fox replied.
"It's all I have."
And I have lived on worse, he said,
and gulped it down with three quick jerks.
Take this. He coughed, then spat a tooth
between my boots. "I thank thee, Fox."

You are most welcome, Human, said
the fox, as formally as I.
He trotted back into the woods.
I walked and didn't think too much
since I was safe. But safe from what,
if anything? Or had I played a part
in some larger design the fox
had put together? I trusted it
— the tooth — because its point was sharp,
because it bore a stain of blood,
because it pricked my finger when
I picked it up. Before or after that,
a deer behind me whispered, *Run!*
I even ran a step or two
before I figured out that *run*
is deer's advice for everything.
I walked two weeks. You're halfway there,
then half of that, then half again,
until you're never there, or till
— May I? — you take a giant step
as in the children's game, cut out
philosophy, and there you are: at home.
Just as my body hit the bed

— in that one instant, flesh on linen —
the whole world shuddered, hesitated, bloomed
so violently, so all-at-once, the house
trembled, and I was frightened that
the walls would fall apart, the roof
explode, the floor dissolve. They held.
The whole house trembled, held — as when,
a child, I sassed my pa in church.
His hand drew back. His whole body
trembled as he kept from hitting me.
And on the fourteenth day, I sagged
into my father's arms. He caught
my weight. I never touched the floor.

II

AFTER THE LOST WAR

After recovering from his collapse, Lanier took the only job he could find in the postwar South — clerk in the Exchange Hotel in Montgomery, Alabama, where he wrote *Tiger-Lilies,* his novel about the war. From Montgomery, he moved back to Macon, married, and finally had to leave his wife and family and go to Texas for his health. After nine months in San Antonio, he returned to Macon, preferring to die young if that was what was necessary for him to be with his family and to pursue his love of music and poetry.

What is the tie 'twixt
mess-pork and poetry?
Lanier

AFTER THE LOST WAR

IN MONTGOMERY — AUGUST 1866

1.

A walk abroad our Sunday streets
is like a stroll through lost Pompeii,
though our lives aren't so interesting
as theirs, at least as Bulwer Lytton tells
of them in his book on the last days.
If you went on a Sunday walk with me,
you'd see that almost nothing moves.
The trees stand motionless, like statues,
and even when a breeze steals in,
the leaves flap once, then idly swing
in dull, half-hearted protest of
the least disturbance of their rest.
Our weekday streets are much like Sunday's,
so business, as you might expect,
sets no one's heart to fluttering.
I don't believe a man in town
could be induced to go into
his neighbor's store and ask, "How's trade?"
He'd have to make amends
for such an insult all his life.
Even the bugs refuse to move
in all this seething heat. Alone
among insects, the bee — beloved
of Virgil for his industry —
is always busy, foraging
even into the midst of town
and seeking out the last coarse rose
or random violet. But then,
after the bees have ceased their toil,
our streets show no life save late in

the afternoon, when girls come out,
slowly, one by one, and shine and move,
as do the stars an hour later.

2.

I don't intend to quarrel with summer.
This is the first since sixty-one
I haven't dressed in butternut.
Yet even in this pastoral land
the green is mixed with battle cries
and phantom groans. A handsome spring
it was. But, my sweet God, to me
the flowers stank of sulphur and
their blooms were flecked with human blood.

At night I think much of the sea.

3.

Come fall I hope to travel north
with the manuscript of *Tiger-Lilies,*
on which I try to work at night,
while moths like dusty knuckles rap
the lighted glass. Before midnight,
when the sultry air is somewhat cooled,
the mockingbirds refuse to sing.
I wait for them. And out my window
the fireflies flicker slower than
I've ever seen those tiny lights.

Our world yawns in a witchery
of laziness. On us is cast

a spell, "an exposition of sleep"
as overtook Sweet Bully Bottom.
The proper term is *aestivation,*
a word that I'm enchanted with.

4.

I've heard they nearly always follow
the river's course — the flaring birds
that arch across the late-night sky
from time to time. I had no way
of guessing what they were: not stars —
though higher than the fireflies rise,
they fly too low for stars. I asked around
and found that drunken sailors set
meat scraps along the riverbanks
and with a crude trap made of rope
ensnare the buzzards they attract.

These birds, kept tied till after dark,
they douse with kerosene, set on fire,
then launch into the evening sky.
The burning makes them fly quite high;
the flying expedites the burning —
it progresses geometrically
until they fall, like burnt-out stars,
into the Alabama River.
One night, preoccupied with work,
I think I made a wish on one.

For them it must be hideous,
but from the ground it's beautiful —

in some odd way an easement of
the savage tedium of days.
But more than that: perhaps you know,
with the younger generation of the South
after the lost war, pretty much
the whole of life has been not dying.
And that is why, I think, for me
it is a comfort just to see
the deathbird fly so prettily.

RAVEN DAYS

These are what my father calls
our raven days. The phrase is new
to me. I'm not sure what it means.
If it means we're hungry, it's right.
If it means we live on carrion,
it's right. It's also true
that every time we raise a voice
to sing, we make a caw and screech,
a raucous keening for the dead,
of whom we have more than our share.
But the raven's an ambiguous bird.
He forebodes death, and yet he fed
Elijah in the wilderness
and doing so fed all of us.
He knows his way around a desert
and a corpse, and these are useful skills.

FIRST ANNIVERSARY

For our first anniversary Father brought by
a bottle of claret. He'd taken it as a fee
from a friend whose cellar had escaped the war.
After he left I found my old horse blanket
— the one thing from the war I wouldn't sell —
and Mary and I went out to drink the wine
in a quiet place we knew beside a stream:
a loaf of bread, a jug of wine, et cetera,
except we left the bread at home.
We stretched out on the blanket, drank the wine,
and as I held her close to me
I smelled the horse-sweat smell of war
drawn from the blanket by our body heat.
It wouldn't scrub out of the heavy wool.
Above our heads and all around the clearing,
their long legs dangling from their potent bodies,
black wasps like armored angels flew,
erratically as flies, drunk on the sweet,
rank scent of scuppernong and honeysuckle.
As we made love, I saw, beyond her head,
a swollen wasp pounce on a caterpillar
and pump her eggs into its yellow skin.
I had to keep my eyes open and watch:
when I closed them the blanket's smell
reminded me of Raven's broken cannon bone
and how I knelt above the heaving mare
and pulled the trigger and walked six miles to camp,
a saddle and the blanket on my shoulder.
Within a week they'll hatch into larvae
and eat the caterpillar from the inside out.

IN SAN ANTONIO

1.

I've left behind the beef-blood cure,
the milk and grape and whiskey cures.
The last displayed some virtues, but
I'm not convinced they were medicinal.
And now I'm on the Texas cure,
the current vogue among us weak of lung.

For health, I'm riding to the West,
as traveling valet to my lungs.
I don't begrudge my death, but loathe
the tending of my namby-pamby flesh —
how it demands my servitude, unlike
when I was young and brutal to this meat.

2.

To His Wife

Though I've been here for fourteen weeks,
my walks have failed to manifest
a singing bird. But blackbirds, Lord!
The local boys stand in their yards
and pot a hundred by the hour.

You know I love the morning woods.
At home, I sit among the pines,
send forth my song, and hear it answered
by larks and other music birds.
Then I pretend that man and nature
are parts of a larger orchestra.
I cannot think that here. But still
I take my flute into the desert

and play as if my solitary tootling
could populate the dawn with birds.

The exercise improves my lungs.

3.

Menger Hotel, Three A.M.

Not halfway through a Schumann piece
a man knocked on my door. He said
my flute disturbed his slumber. He'd
survived the stage from Galveston
and now he needed rest. Would I,
he asked, retire my instrument
so he would not be forced to break
the goddamn thing across his knee.

It stood, I said, a better chance
of being broken on his head.
But still I said I'd put it up.
(He may have been an S.O.B.
but he was clearly in the right.)
When he replied I damn well better,
I responded that I'd changed my mind
and thought I'd play some Wagner next.
We then exchanged such pleasantries
until the manager explained
we could retire *right then*, as strangers,
or he'd request the sheriff come
and introduce us formally.

Next Afternoon

This morning I asked after him
to make apologies. A bellhop said
he'd left upon the early stage.
It's just as well. I doubt he'd let
me beg his pardon gracefully.

4.

Returning home, I stopped the poky roan
beside a mesquite tree, so I
could play my flute and clear my head
of all the fears I have. I'm twenty-nine,
a husband and a father twice,
still lost in games of poetry
and flutes. So I should give it up.
Or make the playing more than play.

Because the flute's a woodland instrument,
I felt incongruous in the desert quiet.
But soon my playing built a decent forest.
It held intact as long as my eyes were closed
and mine was the only sound embroidering
the silence of the afternoon.

Before I got the harmony down pat,
I heard a rhythmic pounding rise
behind my back. Still playing hard,
I stood, and saw along the stream
four women washing piles of clothes.
The dull wet smack of stone on stone
kept steady time. I relaxed, played,

and let my frail notes hurl themselves
against the rhythm of the stones.
Four women turned and glanced at me
with curiosity, then turned away
as though I were superfluous
to any concept they had of the world.
And all the while they held their rhythm:
slow, primitive — slow, loud, and certain.
But as they worked and as I played,
I heard my thoughtless melody
allure them slightly from the beat.

5.

The Meeting of the Männerchor
To His Wife

On the table was much wine and beer,
whereof I quaffed my share, while marveling
at how they sang the *lieder* — brilliantly,
and with such ease. At their request
I lifted my poor flute with great
anxiety and fear. I had
no faith in it or in myself.

Du Himmel, Wife, you should have heard
mine old love warble forth! To my amaze,
I was the master of the instrument.
Is this not strange? Thou knowest what
a botch I made in Marietta
while playing at the Tinsleys' house.
Yet here I ordered forth the notes
and they obeyed. And when I stopped,

Herr Thielepape rose with cheers
and said that he hat never heert
de flude accompany herself pefore!

My love, I was so moved by their kind cheers
and by the song that was so unexpectedly
mine to command, I only smiled and bowed
and smiled and bowed again, although my heart
was working like a mouth about to cry.

6.

At the Livery

To rent my favorite roan, I stopped
and looked for Johnson and his son.
I found them in a back stall, pulling
a chain that ran inside a mare.
She braced herself against their pull,
and moaned. The chain was wrapped around
the ankles of her foal. It was stuck.
Johnson let go. I took the slack.
He reached inside — to elbow, then to armpit —
and yanked the foal. It turned with slippery ease.
The mare fell, eyes huge, her look
more puzzlement than pain. We dragged it out.

It made a smacking sound — like lips.
The foal had strangled on its cord.
Gathered for the afterbirth, the cats
pursued the wheelbarrow out of town.
It doesn't always have to be this way.

7.

Five Sentences from a Letter to His Father,
One a Question

Of course you're right about the money,
but . . .

Some people are unsuited for this world;
it's no surprise I find I'm one.

Father, think how, for twenty years,
through poverty and consumptive bouts,
through the close air of a tiny college,
through service in a threadbare army, prison,
and an exacting business life,
the figures of music and poetry
have clung unto my heart so hard
I couldn't banish them, and only now
have seen I must capitulate.

Does it not seem to you, as me,
that I begin to have the right
to speak without embarrassment
and follow where they lead, these arts
whom I've worshipped long and humbly
and through extended bitterness?

I've work to do I can't do here.

8.

Now that I've made these great resolves
I'm reminded of a story: a frail

graybeard of ninety-plus is set
to wed a robust girl. After debate,
his friends express to him their fears
that the difference in their ages might
prove fatal in the wedding bed.
Tears glistening down his ancient cheeks,
the man replies, "My gentle friends,
I'm moved by your solicitude.
But life is full of risk and loss,
and if she dies, she dies."

THE WORLD OF TURTLES

ON THE GEORGIA COAST

Despite the stink I keep on going back
to watch the giant turtle on the beach.
The sun has not been kind to him
and slowly crabs and gulls are pilfering
the softening flesh from his carapace.
As he is emptied out into the world
the shell is stripped to bric-a-brac,
and those who walk the beach collecting junk
will take it home, shellac it like a gourd,
and set it on a shelf beside a fern.
But what would I do with a living one
flopping around the house and smearing the rug
with slime that smells of week-old fish —
or laying leather eggs beneath the ottoman?
The rubbish the waves deposit on the beach
is all we know of the world of turtles.
What world do they imagine for us
when a careless sailor falls from a ship at sea?
Offshore, a storm is grinding its black teeth.
Tomorrow when I walk the littered beach
the shell and its last scraps of oily flesh
will be washed back to sea. I'll miss my friend.
The ocean though is a serious wilderness.
The black waves race farther up the beach
and start to rock, then lift the turtle shell,
made lighter by its time outside its world.

POSTCARDS OF THE HANGING

1. Clifford, we've grown too far apart.
   So yesterday I bought some postal cards
   and have resolved to send them all to you.
   But what to say? I'm doing well
   and Mary says to say she's doing fine.

2. Remember the large oak beside Halls' barn?
   This afternoon I saw a nigger hanged from it
   for spitting on a white girl's shoes.
   Or so he said. She said he grabbed her breast.
   I suspect the truth is somewhere in between.
   When he said *shoes,* they went berserk.

3. Last night, disturbed, I woke at four o'clock.
   I'd dreamed but couldn't recollect the dream.
   So I got up and studied law
   until I smelled the bacon, eggs, and tea,
   and ate myself into the solid world.

4. In church it hit me like a cannonball:
   I'd dreamed of feet — such gorgeous feet,
   so soft and smooth and dainty pink,
   they looked as if they'd never walked the earth,
   as if they were intended just to walk on air.

5. As far as hangings go, this one was quiet.
   By the time they got him to the tree, they'd calmed.
   They sat him on a mule and slipped the noose
   around his neck. He sang — or started to —
   "Swing Low, Sweet Chariot," but lost his place,
   and when he paused somebody slapped the mule

across the rump. It wouldn't move,
and finally they had to push the mule
from underneath the colored man.

6. The bottoms of his boots were not worn through.
Those boots! They kicked and lashed above the mule
and tried to get a purchase on the air
before they stilled and seemed to stand on tiptoe
like another acorn hanging from the oak.

7. A colored peddler who had stopped to watch
asked them if he could have the dead man's boots.
"He can't use dem, gennelmens," he said.
"And dese ol' boots of mine is shot."
"Why sure, old-timer. Take the boots
and anything else you want off this dead fool."
"I thank ya kindly, gennelmens. Jus' the boots."

8. I blacked my boots after supper tonight —
walking boots, working boots, Sunday shoes,
and even the cavalry boots I wore
when we were living on horseback in the war.
That Raven was a handsome horse!
When I was through, my hands were black
as the dead man's hands. Even my face was smudged.
Now clean, the boots give off an eerie glow
like a family of cats lined up beside the fire.

9. Does this make sense to you? This afternoon
I walked five miles into the woods,
sat down in a clearing in the pines,

and sobbed and sobbed until my stomach hurt.
When I stopped, I tied the laces together,
slung the freshly dirty boots around my neck,
and walked, barefooted, home. When I got there
my feet were sticking to the ground with blood.
It helped a bit. I'm doing better now
and Mary says to say she's doing fine.

REFLECTIONS ON COLD HARBOR

It's after dawn the third of June
— ninth anniversary of Cold Harbor —
and I, who rose before the sun
to walk the darkness from the woods,

am sitting in a neighbor's field
and watching as the early sun
burns off the last dew from the corn.
From men I was in prison with

I heard that Grant's men looked like corn
advancing toward the reaper's blade,
on which they fell relentlessly. That June,

the fields were soaked with summer rain.
If they had actually been corn
we never would have harvested — not wet,
ripe corn. It spoils. As did those men.

Elijah Cobb said that as he fired
into the massive surging of their line
he started crying. Tears blurred his aim.
But he did not withhold his fire:

there were so many running men
that every shot hit something blue,
even a shot fired blind through tears.
He was embarrassed by those tears

and couldn't understand their cause.
And knowing Cobb, a man who once

staged cockroach races for the troops
then ate the winner live, neither can I.

So now I sit amid the corn
and think about the quantities
of fertilizer it requires
— much more than other plants —

and how it's pollinated not by bees
but the vagaries of the summer wind.
The dark sky brightens to deep-ocean blue,
a blue in which some poets have

been known to drown quite happily.
But that's a trick the language plays
with some help from my nervous system
and a human wish to flee the body.

Sometimes, like now, I have great need
to live outside of metaphor,
to know a dawn that's only dawn
and corn that's corn and nothing else.

FISHKILL ON THE CHATTAHOOCHEE

I pushed a dead fish down and held it under.
It wouldn't stay. When I removed my hand
the fish bobbed up, and as I grabbed for it
I stung my middle finger on its fin.
Up close, the fish were a nasty, stinking mess.
I started home but had to turn and look,
and from a distance the acre of dead fish
shimmered like enchanted cobblestones.
From a hill above the Chattahoochee's banks,
I saw the moonlit silver of the fish
catching the light like a length of shining road
that, in another world, had broken free
and drifted down to us with promises
that radiant stones would bear our weight
and the road would lead us to its world.
I forget sometimes the power of the moon.
The unfair beauty of reflected light
made me forget that yesterday the fish
could do more than drift downstream on the current.
But I will tell you this, and it frightens me:
from the hill, removed from individual deaths,
it was the most beautiful thing I've ever seen.
I watched the road and all its borrowed light
move slowly toward the sea — then walked back home,
with care, as though the road beneath my feet
were not as real or solid as I'd thought
despite a drop of blood that fell from my cut,
the blood just barely darker than the clay.

SUFFICIENT WITNESS

When I skip meals, it doesn't bother me.
And Mary, though she's grim, will not complain.
But young boys have to eat. Too often, it's
poke salad, organ meat, red beans and rice.
They whine. I shout. They sulk. I snap at them
and send them off to bed, uncomforted,

their stomachs full. But full of such harsh food
that when I tiptoe in their darkened room
I'm scared to light a match. Cornmeal is cheap.
Dry beans they almost give away. Last night
I cooked the beans again. When Mary saw them,
she cried enormous silent tears

that zigzagged slowly down her face and dropped
into her supper plate. *Go play outside,*
I told the boys, and tried to comfort her.
But what was there to offer — that we'd switch
from pinto back to navy beans? She sobbed
and wouldn't speak. There's also charity.

My neighbor said to take food from his garden.
He said I didn't have to ask. And once I found
a chicken left, still warm, outside the door
before we woke. I crouched there on the porch,
the limp bird cradled in my hands, and wept.
If it were only me I would have kicked

the goddamn bird across the yard and back
to Hobson's house. But Mary and the boys
hurrahed when I brought it to the table stewed,

meat falling from the bones. Another sign:
a yellow dog had come to live with us.
The poor always have dogs. Your income falls

below a certain level and God sends
a hound to comfort you. I've spent whole days
talking with that dumb, suck-egg yellow dog
or pulling broken quills out of its head
as it lay hooked across my thigh. His blood
is flecked across my work pants like a map

of dark red stars. Dog blood. It won't wash out.
Although we cannot feed him, we're his home.
He feeds himself. He roams the neighborhood
and wolfs down windfall apples, grapes, and trash.
He stinks. He steals. He howls at night. He slinks
home rank with bitch on humid summer dawns.

The worse he is, the more I love that dog.
I tell the boys we'll fatten him with beans
and roast him on a spit. *Oh, Diddy, no!*
they yell. We laugh. With feathers from the hen
we ate for supper, I made some corncob darts.
The boys went mad. Screaming like lunatics,

they tossed the darts at Mary, me, the dog,
then heaved them back and forth across the house.
Darts arched across the darkening sky until
they all lodged on the roof. Except for three.
The dog ate one and buried two. Although
the children begged, I wouldn't tell them where.

THE SUMMER OF THE DROUGHT

He wasn't right. We all knew that. His head
bulged oddly on the left above his eye
and he'd eat anything that he could cram
into his mouth. Once, at the creek, I saw
him catching polliwogs and slurping them
out of his palms. I made him stop, of course,
and walked him home, but later he sneaked back,
and Mary saw him down there eating clay.
Then, in the summer of the drought, the streams
dried up, and he crawled underneath my house
to cool down in the dark. I'm guessing now.
He found a wasp nest, grabbed it from the brace,
and stuffed the boiling lump into his mouth.
At least that's what I figure must have happened.
He never talked again. And coming through
the floor beneath my feet, his scream was high
and thin, like flimsy metal being ground.
I was sitting at the table, drinking tea.
The air was heavy with the scent of sulphur
and lilac. I felt it vibrate through my feet.
The human whine of metal being ground.

LISTEN! THE FLIES

I went there early with a bamboo fan,
but every time I paused to greet a friend
the flies would settle back. I'd fan again.
They'd scatter out into the kitchen with

a lazy, slow, resentful tremolo.
It was August — the sort of weather that
makes flies affectionate of flesh
even when it's alive. And Gibson wasn't.

His coffin stretched across four straight-back chairs
set in the parlor. Though he was newly dead,
the flies, prescient, knew he belonged to them.
They find what's theirs: outside the surgeon's tent,

the three-foot hill of amputated limbs
shimmered with flies, as if the whole pile struggled
to pull itself together and walk off —
a beast entirely made of arms and legs.

In prison camp, the flies were fond of us.
I learned to praise the flies. By Gibson's corpse
the preacher had us rise to sing a lie:

"The Green Blade Riseth." I sang along. Although
I've walked the marsh and seen the green blade split
the dried-out clump, I've also been to war.
I know that everything that lives is pitched

from purity to putrefaction, back
and forth. But for the individual corpse

it's permanent. The green blade riseth, yes,
but Mrs. Gibson's Jeff is gone for good.

The Bible doesn't countenance these lies:
from ash to ash, it says, from dust to dust,
with fire and dirty water in between.
Or maybe they are passed to other dust

the way a lie that's passed from ear to ear
might turn into the truth along the way.
I've given this some thought. In winter, mist
rose from the pile as each lopped arm and leg

gave up its fraction of the soul. Last week
a fly got in my room and walked across
my face. The creeping tickle woke me up.
I slapped at it so hard I hurt myself.

Later I got him trapped behind the drapes
and made short work of him. But he'll be back — or one
so much alike it might as well be him.
That changing permanence is what I praise.

AT THE KYMULGA GRIST MILL

The dog runs off to check each breeze
or dashes in a crazy circle.
I don't know what to do with him.
He escorts me all through his woods
as if he's making sure that I
don't change the wild, reclaiming weeds
and vines that pitch themselves across
the few small paths that map his land.
Mine are about the only feet that don't
belong here naturally. The dog is moot —
a beast who's cast his lot with man.

A bright and birdlike fluttering
flashes in the underbrush. A possum corpse
shimmers with orange butterflies.
The dog barks, then charges sloppily.
They scatter, abandoning the rotten flesh
on which they've laid a hundred thousand eggs.
Ten feet or so above the ground
they gather back into a ball
of air and tumbling wings, and roll
erratically across the August river
and past the ruins of an old mill.
The wheel the Chattahoochee turned
lies, fallen, in the shallow water,
which slowly pulls apart the circle
with gentle, almost loving hands.

The roof spreads clumsy covering wings
above the wreckage of the mill — a heap
of rust and rotting wood. Somewhere inside,

a huge imperishable stone remains.
A stone that for a while served man.
Till man withdrew, abandoning the mill
to sedge and sassafras. And now
the mill itself is grist for the mill.

HIS WIFE

My wife is not afraid of dirt.
She spends each morning gardening,
stooped over, watering, pulling weeds,
removing insects from her plants
and pinching them until they burst.
She won't grow marigolds or hollyhocks,
just onions, eggplants, peppers, peas —
things we can eat. And while she sweats
I'm working on my poetry and flute.
Then growing tired of all that art,
I've strolled out to the garden plot
and seen her pull a tomato from the vine
and bite into the unwashed fruit
like a soft, hot apple in her hand.
The juice streams down her dirty chin
and tiny seeds stick to her lips.
Her eye is clear, her body full of light,
and when, at night, I hold her close,
she smells of mint and lemon balm.

A HUSBAND ON THE MARSH

I'm lost. Which is the point. That's why
I come here when I can and walk
the marsh. Well, not exactly lost.
Over scrub pines, I recognize
a cypress that's not too far from the road
back home. I know the marsh too well.
I can't get lost — unlike when I
was just a child. With longer legs,
I see above sawgrass. I know
the stars. I know which side of trees
moss dangles from. I always find
my way back home without much drama.
Or much fear. Even if I stare
into the sun, then close my eyes
and follow the two dots of fire
scored on the back of my eyelids
like stars, I can't get lost. I just
get my feet drenched from stumbling
into water, clothes scuffed from brushing
against trees, my face lashed with limbs,
hands slashed by sawgrass. But when I look
I know exactly where I am.
Or will: This run of rotting fence
connects to Parker's land. This smoke
wafts from a chimney whose fireplace
I've sat by and talked politics.

But I get lost in what it means —
the marsh. Mary just says, "Who cares?"
When I was young I had no doubt
the marsh — the world — was God's mind. We

were God's thoughts as we trampled through
the bog, fished, hunted deer, and tried
to keep our awe in check. Why try?
But then I started in on meaning,
which goes nowhere. So then I thought
that play was all there was to it —
not least because, out wandering,
I've seen the red-tailed hawks I love
scream in midair on windy days
until, God-like, the male bird tucks
his wings and plummets toward his mate.
A scant half second before he hits,
he spreads wing and zooms off. Repeatedly
he feints, then veers, as I watch noon
sunlight glow red through his tail feathers.
And once, as he bore down, I saw
the female flip. The two locked talons
and tumbled almost to the pines before
they separated and the game
resumed. Courtship! I loved it once.
But who could bear it every spring?
Well, Mary could. "Don't be so serious,"
she says. But play is not enough.
I'm of at least two minds — like one
strange salamander that I found.
These salamanders breed too fast
to do it well — three tails, six legs.
With heads at either end, it crawled
one way until that end collapsed,
and then the other end would crawl
the other way — till it collapsed.

I tried to let it go. But how
could it escape? I tossed it back
into the mud and left it there, alive
when I walked off, but after that,
who knows? I'm stuck with stories now.
Perhaps this is a better one:
Along the Chattahoochee's bank,
I saw green cankerworms, in thousands,
moil — seethe — beneath the cottonwoods
like fat, green, severed fingers searching
for their lost hands. A scene of hell,
one Dante overlooked. But later,
at night, I went again and found
the cankerworms were gone. Instead
an equal number of dust-brown
moths fluttered over water. They
turned white, then silver, transformed
by moonlight. Exquisite. I left before
the magic turned them back to moths.

But here, lost, when I could get lost,
I loved the idea of mosquitoes,
lice, and ticks living off my blood,
as I lived off the meaning of the marsh.
Or off its lack of meaning — back
and forth. Mosquitoes, ticks: I loved
them as ideas. I never felt
so thoroughly that I was just
a soul and nothing else than when
my body fed their bodies. But,
dammit, the actual fact of them

was more than I could bear. They *hurt.*
But I've told Mary what to do
with facts: smack them around, and see
if they will tell you anything.
Some do. Some don't. Some waffle. Hell,
she's not convinced.

In winter light,
the marsh is stark, abstract. Just up
and down. The hard-edged light is clear,
incisive as a razor blade.
In summer, that same light smears everything.
Trees waver. Bushes merge into
a haze of gnats, shimmering in air,
which shimmers too — the whole world dizzy
and unsure. Meaning falls away.
The brilliant winter light, which then
made everything seem clear, now lies.
Or for the first time tells the truth.
Who cares? I do. But Mary loves me
whether I'm hawk, worm, salamander,
moth, tick, or just a confused man,
apprentice to himself, who fails
to grasp the meanings of the light,
although he loves them both: the winter light,
the summer light. And Mary too.

III

FLAUTO PRIMO

After accepting a position as first flautist with the Peabody orchestra, then one of the finest in the country, Lanier at first lived in lodgings in Baltimore and returned to Macon when the orchestra season ended. Toward the end of his life, he bought a house and moved his family north to be with him.

FLAUTO PRIMO

Amid the orchestra, I thrill
to ride the larger surge. Sometimes
I thrill so much I lose my place.
Not often. A man with dwindling lungs
the flauto primo! I disappear
inside the other instruments
and doubly hide in my own flute,
as breath that sweeps the centuries
and scours millennia lifts me
and carries me a year or two
per fretum febris through the straits
of fever and the channels of
the flute, King David's instrument,
the shepherd's working tool, and, further,
to Orpheus, who almost — almost! —
restored the dead by playing well.
My brother says that when I play
I'm dead to this world. Sometimes that
is where I need to be, as if
I'm scouting out infinity.
I disappear, invisible
inside the flute, like a dead soldier
who's learned, at last, to march in step.
If Brother doesn't understand,
hooray! Although he's never learned
to keep the count — left, right; left, right —
he fought as wickedly as I
and killed almost as many men.
Inside the instrument, I find
brief sanctuary where there is
no death — almost no death — until

my awe veers out beyond control.
I stumble, gasp — a tremor through
the canticles of breath — and then
the whole song crashes into flawed,
harsh finitude. But for a time
what leaves my mouth as used-up breath
flies from the flute, determined to
be something else, as when you slam
your fist against your eyes: the pain
produces light, then brighter light
and still more light the harder that
you jerk your fist into your eyes —
the blood-light shocked, in flashes, from
the pain the body gives itself.
And if it isn't really light, it's light
to the one sense that uses light.

APPETITE FOR POISON

1.

Baltimore

We men in lodgings, after supper,
rush out to walk the streets. They're jammed
with restless men seeking privacy
in mass. I know it doesn't make much sense.
And many find their way to brothels
where, for a couple of dollars,
they shed their loneliness awhile
in a way that makes them lonelier.
I saved up for a month. I went
to a whorehouse so exorbitant
the whores were likely to be clean,
less jarring on the sensibilities.
It's strange how lust makes you confront
appearance and reality.
Consider the woman that I chose:
she had the looks a man like me
gets moony over — and intellectual eyes.
She said she was Marie-Louise.
But when she talked she sounded worse
than any hayseed I've ever heard.
The girls there all have fake French names.
My God, she was a handsome child!
But when she had to say something,
even great beauty didn't help.

At work, I asked the second flute
what his wife would do if she found out
he'd been with other women. He grinned,
nudged, winked, and slashed his index finger
across his throat — then laughed so hard

I thought the fool would hurt himself.
It's as though I had acquired, somehow,
an appetite for poison.

2.

Last fall, right after Sid was born,
we made love once. Since then,
Mary's refused to sleep with me.
Each night before we went to bed,
she'd peck me quickly on the cheek,
tiptoe into the boys' bedroom,
and sleep on a pallet on the floor.
It was a hard birth. Two days' labor.
Some nights I'd go and check on her
as she slept curled up like a child,
and on those nights it was as if
I had three children — two boys
and this new ghostly, troubled girl.
To hold her would have been too close
to sin. So I would watch her sleep,
amazed at how completely *other*
she was. I'd ache for her, for all
the strength she'd given me.
And, now, for once, I had my health
and I would place my hand against
her shoulder blade, and concentrate,
trying to force my health on her.
To hold her would have been too close.

Days, she was my wife again. Except
when I walked up and slipped my arms

around her waist. Her torso stiffened,
as though the slightest touch would lead
to bed, to sex, to birth, to all
the blood she lost in having Sid.
(We had to throw the mattress out.)
I'd let go. She'd recoil. And we'd
stand awkwardly, embarrassed, till
we found something we could turn to,
some task. She wouldn't talk about it,
denied that anything had changed.
As if Sid's birth weren't hard enough,
the last time we made love, I had
a spasm in my lungs and spit
blood on the pillowcase. Not much.
Right after that, we took a walk
and saw the body of a cow. It buzzed,
the whole corpse vibrant with a hum,
the whine of deep machinery.
From holes beneath the tail, bees came
and went. Inside, the unseen wings went wild,
pitched higher and higher, as if
they strained to lift it off the ground.
I thought for a moment I'd throw up.
And Mary calmly turned away,
took two short steps, and fainted in my arms.

A last excuse (it isn't very good):
I am alone in Baltimore
and she's in Georgia with the boys.

3.

Perhaps another story helps:
I had a Leghorn cock that would
couple with anything. The hens
acquired a chafed, bowlegged walk.
It was lamentable to hear
them shrieking as the eggs scraped out.
I often had to grab a broom
and swat him off the other poultry,
the sow, and even, once, the mule.
One afternoon I saw a buzzard
circling the rise beyond the barn,
and when I went to look I found
the cock stretched out atop the rise,
flat on his back, claws rigid in the air.
The buzzard flew tight circles, interested.
I thought the stupid cock had humped
itself to death. Quite literally.
But when I bent to pick him up
he whispered in my ear, *Hold on,*
the buzzard's just about to land!

I guess it doesn't clarify
much of anything. The joke
is old and everybody's heard it.
But I have thought of it a lot
lately. I nearly always laugh,
a guilty laugh, of course. But still . . .

Hold on, it's just about to land!

4.

I started sobbing as my face plunged
over her shoulder. She was kind
and said that many clients cried.
I doubt it's true. I don't believe
most men are foolish as I am.

My heart's not in that sort of thing,
but flesh drags everything along
with it — even the puling conscience.
When I went back the second time
I screwed and screwed but didn't come.

Marie was tired and grouchy, dry
and bored. I told the little snip
I was entitled to my money back.
She was astoundingly foul of mouth
and unpersuaded. *Caveat emptor.*

Sin is just part of it. Money's
the other part: the mortal sins
are cheap, the venial ones cost money.
I could have sent the dollars home
to Mary and the boys. It took

a month of watching tone-deaf brats
act up, and slobber in their flutes,
and drain the slobber on my rug.
I've never known a single thing
that money doesn't complicate.

5.

Macon, Georgia

Last Sunday night when I got home
— the concert season being over —
Mary slid into bed with me at three
and wanted to make love. We did.
It's over. Whatever it was.
We'll have someone to sleep next to
on Georgia August nights — so hot and still —
and into old age and beyond.
I don't know how it came to end.
Sometimes it's better not to ask.

6.

After she'd started to show last spring
we went out for a midday spin.
When I suggested it, she got
excited as a little girl —
put on her new white frock and thumped
her Easter bonnet on her head.
I kept the rented carriage slow.
We'd been out almost an hour
when a sharecropper left his mule
and walked beside us for a quarter mile
before he spoke. He asked me if
"the lady" felt like planting his
first handful of seed corn. It is
good luck, apparently, to have
a pregnant woman start your crop.
His shyness touched her. Gingerly,
she tiptoed through the red, plowed field,

sticky with rain and slick as lard.
To me, it looked too wet for planting.
She started to bend down, but slipped,
fell to her knees. He really should
have waited till the ground was dry.
But Mary was meticulous.
She spaced the kernels carefully
and pinched the red clay over them.
When she stood up her hands and smock
were red. She was more bloody than
any surgeon I remembered from the war,
though she resembled them — the way
she held her hands out from her sides
as if she didn't want to touch herself.

I tried to turn the farmer down
but he insisted that we take a gift —
"Won't work if I don't pay you back."
I took a gourd. And Mary held it on
her lap and joked that in two months
she'd look exactly like the gourd.
And I leaned over, kissed her cheek.
Back home, I cut an opening in the gourd,
dumped out the mass of seeds, and hung
it from the shagbark hickory.
At dusk, in summer, I like to watch
the purple martins swoop over the pines
and shoot into the opening,
unerring and precise as, well,
a purple martin to his gourd.
While we sat on the porch one evening

— this after Sid was born — we saw
a martin hit a dragonfly so hard
it snapped the body from between the wings.
They flickered slowly to the ground,
caught light, and flashed like airborne mica.
Mary walked over, found the wings,
and shut them in her locket. I'm not sure why.
But I had also wanted them.

MEMORIES OF LOOKOUT PRISON

When John grew ill and couldn't eat,
I almost stole his corn. The bowl
sat by his tossing head for more
than fourteen hours. No one,
no one at all was watching me.
I tried to spoon it in his mouth.
He pushed my hand away. Later,
I forced a spoonful past his lips
and had to rake it out again
when he refused to swallow. I tried
to make him eat that goddamn mush.

I did not steal this bowl of corn.
But, Christ, I wanted to, which Paul
says is the same as doing it —
a sin I made so often and
so vividly inside my head
I sometimes think I ate the mush.
I grieve as if I had. Of course
it's not the same to John, who got
just well enough to choke it down
before he died. But to my soul,
if there is any of it left,
St. Paul was right: the sin is made.

In the war I thought to lose an arm
or leg. Not what I lost. Not that.
The Bible says that ye shall know
the truth. It doesn't say the truth
will tear you, ruthless, limb from limb.

THE HOUSE ON DENMEAD STREET

When I walk down the street — *my* street —
a certain burgher heaviness
weighs in my tread. Why skip along
like the bohemian I was
just months ago? I am, like you,

a man of property. I'm through
with grieving over money. O,
the goddamn shekel, the almighty buck.
The shop clerks knew. They sniffed at me
as if I had rank canker sores

that only they could smell. Last spring,
when I walked past MacAuley's store
I'd stare at this one pair of boots.
Pearl gray. And butter soft. Sometimes
I'd go inside and touch the deep,
rich suede. They were such gaudy boots!

I longed for them as if my soul
were somehow twined around their thingness.
Now, I'm amazed at how, beneath
my desire, those poor bastard things
became no longer shoes. Instead

they changed to symbols of my life,
as if I'd stumbled, unaware,
into a Dickens serial.
But then the shop clerk cleared his throat
and sneered. I blushed and left the store,

went home, sat down, ignored my verse,
and wrote more trash for currency:
The Boy's King Arthur, histories, and
a travel book on Florida,
a state I'd like to visit once

and see how close to actuality
I'd come.
In one way — clothes — these are
good years for poverty. Each spring
another woman in the town
gets up the nerve and gives to charity

her husband's or her son's old clothes —
another benefit of the war.
What dream of property can slow
the sullen lock step of the heart
toward death: brick house, wood house, straw house?

Who cares? I *own* my house, eight rooms
on Denmead Street in Baltimore,
in Maryland, America,
the planet Earth, the mind of God.
From firmament to fundament,

I own a fine, substantial house
and, with it, whitewashers, locksmiths,
gas-fitters, plumbers, piano-movers,
and carpet-layers — and all the dignity
of being liable for their bills.

FEVER

The constant simmer in my lungs
burns differently in different places.
On the autumn coast at Wilmington,
marsh fevers used our bones for dice
and rolled those bones against our lives.
It was a different sort of fever

from the dry shakes of the sand hills.
As a child in Georgia I was prone
to gentle spells of hot and cold
that rocked me through both day and night
and made me think about the flux
of sunlight in our daily lives

and how my fevers contradicted it
so I was often hot at night
and chilly in the heat of day.
Because of this, I was a dreamy child,
not fond of games and other boys.
I couldn't bring my mind to bear

on what we humans mean to one another,
and I'm afraid I learned of that
from *Adam Bede* and *Middlemarch.*
But here, in Baltimore, the fevers seem
to want to tell me things.
After a night of cold, I had

a night of burning, sweat, and dreams
— my fifth night in a row like this —
and as I left the final dream

I saw a sort of explanation
of my war with geography.
It was that all men draw from earth

a spark of fire and a spike of cold
that ought to cancel one another.
Some men can't bring the two together
and split their lives between extremes.
But now it's day. I'm cold again.
I don't understand my understanding.

HE IMAGINES HIS WIFE DEAD

I'd just leapt quickly to the curb
to keep from being run down by a horse,
when suddenly I understood my wife might die,
and since that time I've thought of little else,
as if the threatened mind is trying
to keep from being taken by surprise.
And worse, it tries to find the benefits:
the joys of flirting and games of courtship —
all things I loved but have no use for now.
How can I blame the mind? It wants to live
and will be ruthless to that end,
as a plant that's moved into a darkened room
will drop the lower, inessential leaves
to keep the growing tip alive. But the heart
depends on more than blood. It needs a cause.
I left my dull heart beating when I slept,
and found it beating when I woke
to Mary smiling oddly in her fever
as she lay tangled in the sweaty sheets.
Her eyes, unfocused and afraid,
were a blue I'd never seen in eyes before,
as if a jay were caught inside her head
and through her eyes I saw it leaping back and forth
and trying to extend its bright blue wings.
It scared me more than prison camp or war.
My Mary is my only love
that's not a subterfuge for death.

A RAPPROCHEMENT WITH DEATH

I knew for sure on January seventeenth.
I woke with my mouth full of blood.

I start the new year with a certainty
which heretofore had been a fear.

My life is balanced on my lungs
the way an anvil rests upon an egg:

it takes a gentle touch to keep it there.
And in my sleep I dream of birds.

A mockingbird at night bodes death
and I suppose I'm straining for his song

when I should be in bed asleep —
and dreaming of a mockingbird.

I can't escape these harbingers,
so, like the January sun,

which holds a brilliant spike of chill,
I need to forge a rapprochement with death

to balance off the ecstasy and terrors —
that's one ecstasy and many terrors.

And like a dark red boat on a scarlet sea
I'll sail whatever ocean holds me up.

GLYPHS

I sleep on messages I've left
myself, then wake to new ones slanting
across the day-before's. Each day
I scrub the Latin back to beige.
Each night I write on it in red,

the logos of the body bright
on wedding cambric. In back of it
the Greek of ancient prophecy
sinks deeper in. I mostly get
the sense but miss the nuances.

Perhaps it's more like cuneiform,
of which I know nothing. The body
itself is Babylon, its glyphs
tell how, in foreign wars, the king
brought back a hundred thousand slaves,

gold, flocks of sheep, and cypress beams,
whose scent was good. They boast of kings,
of Nebuchadnezzar, who built
his wife a wonder of the world.
A garden so rich in the magic

of slaves, it floated in midair.
But even Nebuchadnezzar writhed in
the dirt, ate grass, and needed a Daniel
to read the MENE TEKEL on the wall.
Each prophecy hunts down and claims

its prophet. What am I to make
of what I scrub off my pillowcase?

Or these red glyphs I see each day:
a scarlet chevron on the black-
bird's wing, the blood-streaked lily and

the flecks of coughed-up lung that hang
suspended in my spit. Mary
no longer cries. She's all cried out.
Her Latin's good as mine, her Greek
superior. We do not talk.

A FATHER ON THE MARSH

My older boy said, "Let's make soup."
Like a damn fool I said okay.
As Chuck and I circled the cooter,
my youngest, Sid, jammed both his thumb
and his index finger in his mouth,
something he hadn't done for months.
The cooter tucked its head and flippers.
I jabbed its armpit with a stick.
Its beaked head flickered out, eyes slit,
malevolent. *"Stand back,"* I yelled. The boys
stumbled behind a fallen log
but never looked away. I said,
"If loggerheads bite you, they won't
let go until it thunders." Chuck
said, "Is that true?"
                                        "Let's not find out,
okay?" The green head darted, snapped.
I lashed the ax through its thick neck.
The lopped-off head still snapped. Set free,
the body lunged into the grass
as if it didn't need a head.
Sid screamed. I sliced the top shell off
and all the turtle's guts, compact
and pulsing, opened to our view,
much like the workings of a watch,
except the boys were more enthralled
than they'd be with a watch. A watch
won't bite or battle. A watch won't die.
They stared into the throbbing, raw
insides I'd opened. And then,
for the first time — too late — I asked,

What have I done to my boys? Although
I couldn't eat the thick green soup,
they did. They slurped it down without,
I guess, a thought about the cooter.
But I was that way too.

My first
shot missed the stag, and Father fired
just as it broke for cover. It
made two huge bounds before collapsing
into scrub brush. Field-dressing it,
we found a madstone in its guts —
a fist-sized chunk of calcium,
deer pearl. You soak it in warm milk,
then press it on a wound to draw
the heat or poison out. "Save this,"
my father said. "Save it. You'll need
a little magic in your life."
He laughed. But while the boys slept late,
their bellies full of turtle soup,
I walked out on the winter marsh.
The wind slashed at my face all morning,
then stopped. Just stopped. Or so I thought,
until I saw it snatching at
brown clumps of grass beside the path.
I held my right hand out, the palm
turned flat against the wind, which pounced on it.
The same thing happened on the left.
By chance, I'd found an island in
the shifting wind, an opening.
I laughed out loud and almost prayed
to live like that — outside the blast.

But men with two boys and one coming
know better than to waste a prayer
on the impossible. I stood
a long time in the tempting calm
— until the island whipped away —
then I walked home into the wind,
leaning against its blade, which held me up.

THE YELLOW STEEPLE

On my way home from work, I jumped the fence
and cut across the Baptist cemetery.
As I walked over Sarah Pratt,
I saw a workman standing on a scaffold
and swatting a coat of yellow paint
over the peeling whitewash on the steeple.
He dropped a can of paint, and as it fell
the paint dispersed into a mist
and spread a rain of yellow dots
across a corner of the cemetery —
the bushes, trees, headstones, and me.
It ruined my coat. I didn't care:
I felt like Danae when she
was loved by Zeus in the golden rain.
Then, looking up, I saw a hawk.
It didn't move at all — not once —
but hung arrested in the air
till I released the breath I held
in awe of its pinpoint, predatory grace.
Still watching it as I walked home,
I barked my shins on a marble angel,
slid down a bank of slick white mud,
fell in the creek, and came up laughing.

It was one of those sustaining days
when you're absolutely sure you have a soul.

IV

UNDER CANVAS

In 1881, Lanier's health failed utterly. In a desperate attempt to prolong his life, he and his family moved to the mountains of North Carolina and set up Camp Robin, named after their youngest child. Sidney Lanier died on Wednesday, September 7, 1881, at ten A.M. As he weakened, his wife offered him a drink of cherry cordial. He said, "I can't," and died shortly afterward without speaking again.

A CHRISTIAN ON THE MARSH

In May, I can't see dogwood bloom
without thinking how it was once
as huge as hickory — till Christ
was nailed to one. Since then, dogwoods
are twisted, small. A legend. A lie.
But I can't get it from my mind.
That's not the only lie I've seized:
I've heard a preacher say the dead,
in heaven, watch our every move.
It's dumb. But I think I believe it.
You'd think they'd find a better way
to waste eternity. What do they *feel*
as they look down from heaven and judge
the part of me that isn't earth?
I know the earth desires me back,
desires the part of me that's earth —
and I'm not sure how much that is,
despite the mud-suck at my ankles
that's luscious, sexual. I love
the way my footprints fill with seepage
and crumple back into sea level.
Just twenty years ago, I saw
a heelprint fill with human blood.
Not mine. I could forget it if
the blood were mine. I'm dangerous.
As I chug through the mud, a bird,
a killdeer, dragging one dropped wing,
decoys me from her nest. Spring peepers sing,
knee deep, knee deep. I sing it back.
Our voices meld, then separate.
When I was still too young for school,
I watched the wheelwright making wheels.
In fire, he stretched a thick iron strap,

then bent it on a wooden wheel,
which immediately began to smoke
and char. Then he grabbed it, and pitched
the smoldering wheel into his pond.
The hot iron whistled, chuckled, sighed,
and clamped, skintight, against the wood.
The whole idea was permanence,
my father said. I said "Yes, sir,"
but even then I understood
it wasn't permanence, but time.
Even the fine red Georgia dust,
in time, wears through the iron. It's strange
how everything I say becomes
a symbol of mortality,
a habit I cannot resist
and don't care to.

Fragranced with cedar,
a slight wind rustles in the reeds,
and as in Ovid and in Chaucer
they whisper *aures asinelli* — asses' ears —
and who am I to disagree
with Ovid, Chaucer, or the reeds
when they say I'm a fool to search
for symbols of my fate. But — fool
or not — I still probe the salt marsh
as priests three thousand years ago
searched entrails for a sign. It's hard
to face death and remain sophisticated,
so I don't try.

As I walked on,
the field was chock-a-block with starlings.
They packed each green bush, large and small,

as if they were its natural fruit,
and spread across the ground so thick
I barely saw a blade of grass.
A tremor ran among the birds.
The cause of their distress, a hawk,
was high and watchful in the sun.
With a perfunctory swoop, he feinted
at one shrub thick with birds. They rose
en masse before the hawk got near.
He veered off and they settled back
with loud congratulations for
their neat escape: *Kee you! Kee you!*
Once more a scare ran through their ranks.
They raised their wings, began to fly,
but in that half a second as
they struggled for a grip on meager air,
the hawk exploded in their midst
and turned a somersault in flight,
his talons clamped on one slow bird.
I sat shaken — astonished and afraid,
but also moved — by this assurance that
God keeps his eye on everyone
and snatches even those who flee his grace.
The hawk, though, didn't carry off his prey.
He hunched, and ate it in the field
while all creation stopped, or so it seemed,
to watch him rip deliberately
the stringy entrails from its gut.
In that, he wasn't much like God
— I hoped, as I walked deeper in
the darkening marshes past my home,
through clover, chamomile, under heaven.

THE CULT OF THE LOST CAUSE

Camp Robin, Near Asheville
August, 1881

Dear Clifford — caballero, brother —
Thanks for the good luck charm. Whose teeth
bit these marks in the lead? Not yours?
Is it something you found, or did
somebody pass it on to you?
I trust the poor man lived, and not
too badly crippled, either. There's
not much good luck and little charm
in the one-legged men we could have been.
We've talked of this. But I've discovered
another fact: in '66
the state of Mississippi spent
one-fifth of all state revenues
on artificial limbs. And here,
in Asheville, our hot streets sway with
the tick-tock walk of crippled men.
I've held — you must have known I would —
the bullet in my mouth, and bit.
I clenched until my jaw throbbed. Now,
the bullet's mine: my practice bite
obliterates the first one there.

When they came in — the lists of dead
and wounded — which did you read first?
Though I could look across the camp
and see you drinking acorn coffee,
combing snarled thistles from your mount,
or frying mush, I'd always check
to make sure you weren't on the lists —

first dead, then wounded. Night fell. Tired men
and horses drifted, one by one,
to sleep. Dung streamed down horses' hocks,
green as pea soup. In spring, wind-whipped
green leaves would not let me drift off,
and then they would. Fall came. The last
leaves on the limb flailed — intermittent, frantic —
like limed birds stuck upon a twig.
Then it was day again. We'd rise,
grab rifles, dash into the stink
of sulphur and saltpeter, where, amid
the orders of the captains and the shouting,
boys who had conjugated Latin verbs
were conjugated likewise into death,
which is, I guess, the future perfect tense.
And boys who'd fought the Gallic wars
now limp the streets of Beulah Land.
They walk long-short, long-short, and mock
the Latin line, their bodies swaying to
the music of dead languages.
I'm sick of our lost cause — the way
it's talked about, as if, beneath
sweet words for suffering, we weren't
fucked Ivanhoes of wickedness.
Moonlight, magnolias, mournful songs
of darkies working in the fields:
for some these memories are happy.
Sometimes, before I catch myself,
I'm one of them. I've come to hate
the lost cause and the cult of Beulah.
Bear with me. I've pushed back this guilt

for twenty years and now I indulge it.
God didn't make us out of clay
by chance: we mark that easily.
But now I feel like the Tar Baby,
walking through life with everything
I've ever done or thought about
glued to my flesh. Forgive my anguish.
People make fun of me, you know,
for being so damn serious.
When we first met, Mary complained,
"Why's everything a joke to you?"
Now it's "Don't be so serious."
I try. But when I tease, her face
almost crumples in tears and then
she catches herself at the sob
and tries to laugh. She knows, and thinks
I don't. She tries to keep it from me.
We barely talk, so rich are we
with death and lengthy silences,
infinitude and paradise,
where it is always harvest time:
no planting, weeding, fear, or drought,
just harvest, harvest, harvest, all
year long. That's one possibility,
the one that Mary likes. But she's
a gardener. She works all day
while I lie in my tent, write you,
and read my botany. For years,
I've been forbidden to pitch hay
or swing an ax or nine-pound sledge,
but now I'm not allowed to hoe,

walk half a mile, or play my flute.
And Mary's strict about these *don'ts*.

The bullet makes her angry. Don't
be hurt. She fears I've given up
on God and prayer, and moved backward
to superstition. But she's wrong.
I've always trusted numens, signs —
believed the spirit in the thing
communicates with us. *Believed*
is too strong. Let's say *hoped* instead.
Remember when we visited
that Negro fortuneteller? Though
I can't recall the prophecies,
I can't forget her fingers on my head
and how they loved the bumps, caressed
irregularities — as if she read
the *Iliad* across my skull.
On top, she traced a long, deep crease.
"Peach head," she said. You laughed. *Peach head!*
Peach head! For months you called me that.
For months you asked if I'd been back
to the peach tree I'd been plucked from.
You jollied me, and teased. I snarled.
This was when I was feverish,
my weak head lolling on your shoulder.
You held me up. You marched for me.
Then you fell ill and I, in turn,
held your limp body upright, as
we marched and staggered through Virginia.
Though it was misery, I have

found comfort in that memory.
It has sustained me — like your grip.
We both wrote of the war. Two men,
two books. When I went North with mine,
the Yanks talked of their victory.
What could I do? Talk of defeat?
Or prison? I couldn't tell the Yanks,
goddammit, that I was glad we lost.
I nodded, sipped my drink, and burned.
Forgive me, I am glad we lost.
Relieved. Or I'm glad my side lost
and sorry your side also lost.

So serious! Forgive. Let's talk
of funerals. Do you recall
when Uncle Walter died? In August,
two hundred mourners packed a church
designed for fifty. The fainting started early,
and you and I, just boys, helped tote
the fainting men and women out.
Then we removed our drenched suit coats
and fanned them back to consciousness.
Although we lugged limp bodies, dripped
with sweat, and almost fainted too,
we never once stopped singing hymns.
And Walter's son came late — and drunk —
and tripped, face down, into the aisle.
He rolled onto his back, belched twice,
and never missed a note. He had
a gorgeous drunken baritone.
Is this all gospel? Or am I
romanticizing things again?

I can't understand those folks
who say they wouldn't change a thing.
Except for you, the boys, and Mary, I'd
change everything. And I forgive
only because I have no choice,
because there *is* no changing things.
And even prayer can't change the past,
which doesn't stop my trying to
each night. And, Clifford, once, in fever,
I prayed to you — a tiny sin,
perhaps, but I am fond of it.
Please sing "Lead Kindly Light." Don't grieve.
Don't wash my corpse or trim my beard.
These August days are excellent for corn,
but I prefer cool autumn days,
when I can't see bright red or yellow leaves
without thinking, *That's how I'd like to die:*
that flowering of something that can't flower.

THE LIGHTNING TREE

While Mary rakes the coals, leans fatwood chips
on the weak glow, and starts the fire again,
the morning sun streaks through the hickory
we've camped beneath. Thick green leaves splinter light
to thin diagonals. For mountain air,
we've moved back to the Alleghenies, where
I spent the spring of '61. Then, too,
I lived inside a tent, slept on the ground
as it grew softer, bouncy, with new growth.

In April, we pitched borrowed army tents
beneath a lightning tree. When we got here,
a tuft of bear fur fluttered on the bark.
Up close, I caught the scent of bear without
the bear's great heat, the patch of fur still rank
with the bear stink of he who left it here.
I took this as a sign.
                                        Fire, twice, had gouged
loose spirals down the shagbark trunk, ripped round
the wide bole, widdershins, and scarred the wood,
making, as it scorched down, one and a half
fierce revolutions of the trunk. Amazed,
I ran my fingers up the scars, as far
as I could reach. One track, the newer one,
still sticky, held a spider trapped in resin.
This also I took as a sign. Of course.
And so did Mary. "It's a sign all right,"
she said. "And not a good one. Look here, Sid,
that's Celtic thought. You're thinking like a Druid
or some red Indian." I kissed her, laughed,
and she gave in.

And, really, what's the chance
another bolt will blast the hickory
and slam into my tent? Not much, I think.
But who can tell when they'll come or what
they mean — these strange, impersonal violences
that nature gives us? Just last spring, the boys
roused me from *A Midsummer Night's Dream:* "Diddy,
come look! Come look!" I followed them — all four —
down to the garden. A white-tailed doe,
her head trapped tight inside the barbwire fence,
lunged on the strands. On tiptoe, I slid up
and tried to separate the wire. Three times,
so quick it seemed a single blow, the doe's
rear hooves lashed out and thudded on my chest.
Knocked back, I stumbled, fainted, fell
among the boys, and then came to. They cried.
Sid threw a large stone. It made a hollow sound
against the doe's side. She shook violently,
jerked free, slipped twice as she began to run,
then vanished — poof! — into the nearby pines.
I promised them a beating, a serious beating,
if they told Mama. Then I winked. They laughed
and wiped their tears, sucked noses dry, and said
they understood. I hope not. But for weeks
I pressed my fingertips into the bruises,
tracing the pain, as black-gray blotches turned
blue, shaded into yellow stains — much like
the nicotine between my father's fingers —
before they faded back to pink. Each time
the pain grew less, so I pushed harder still
to find the same bright pain I knew was there

beneath the rainbowed skin. And, from inside,
I felt the fingers of my breath push back.
They also probed. They also pressed against
the membrane separating in from out
and out from in. And when the bruises healed
and I stopped probing at their world,
the inside fingers grew insistent, as if
they missed me, wondered where I'd gone, and why
I'd stopped searching for them. As time's gone on,
they've turned less gentle. Sometimes, they
rack me, as if, like Madeline Usher, they'd
been buried alive and I were their grave,
and they, determined, were clawing their way out.

Later I walked back to the fence and peeled
the bloody brown hair off the barbs. Perhaps
I planned to work a mojo, a hoodoo.
But I don't know how. Or maybe I do.
I woke this morning with an erection.
What am I, a dying man, to do with it,
except admire the irony?

Although it's been twice struck, the tree's thick leaves
shine just as bright as those on other trees.
Squirrels scrabble on its branches, gossiping
and hurling nuts that thud arhythmically
against the drum-taut canvas of our tents.
Inside the greenery, invisible,
a flicker drums the bark for grubs, flies hum,
a wood thrush flutes. A morning breeze wafts in
a distant skunk smell, and it lifts, in passing,

the bear tuft clinging to the bark. Pans clank.
From seasoned hickory, the flames break free
and stretch, luxuriate — fire polishing
itself, catlike; and sparks jump from its fur
as if, lighter than air, they had no weight,
no weight at all.

And, literarily,
Mount Pisgah, North Carolina, hulks
in distant mist. Around the world from us,
the Himalayas are still rising. Mary
shouts "Rise and shine," not knowing I, awake,
have watched her every move. She calls again,
brings me a cup of tea, and kisses me.
The tea steams in the sharp dawn air. She waits.
I sip tea rich in sugar, rich in cream.
She pats my leg and marches to the spot
she's chopped into the underbrush
for vegetables. The bees already are at work.
From here, I hear the rising hum. I could,
if I limped over and listened to her fuss,
inspect the yellow powder smeared like gold
across the legs and abdomen. She grows
just vegetables. She wants me to eat well,
and heal. But as we drove through town last month,
the jasmine, jonquils, and forsythia,
and even, yes, the daffodils, were up.
I can't think of another year in which
the yellow flowers bloomed in such heart-rich
profusion. In this bright, coiled bulb of pain
beneath my collarbone, another flower

is opening. I feel it bloom. As yet,
I'm not sure what it is, but I would bet
a daffodil — the yellow bloom I love most.

I sip the rest of my rich, lukewarm tea
and think, *This place is almost paradise.*
A sweat bee, drawn to the dregs of tea,
backstrokes the air above my cheeks and plays
his feelers on my skin. When he discerns
I'm flesh, he jilts me for a jimsonweed
and riots in its sugar and its drug.
I watch, just barely jealous — as, last night,
I watched the moon. I studied it until,
like the blade of a well-honed ancient scythe,
it spun from my sight, harvesting the stars,
the darkness, night, and all the trembling,
hushed leaves of hickory it swung into.

How strange to live upon a spinning globe!

WHAT LIGHT DESTROYS

Today I'm thinking of St. Paul — St. Paul,
who orders us, *Be perfect.* He could have said,
Touch your elbow to your ears, except
that if you broke your arm, then snapped your neck,
you might could manage it. The death inside
the flawed hard currency of what we touch
bamboozles us, existing only for that flaw,
that deathward plunge that's locked inside all form,
till what seems solid floats away, dissolves,
and these poor bastard things, no longer things,
drift back to pure idea. And when, at last,
we let them go we start to pity them,
attend their needs: I almost have to think
to keep my own heart beating through the night.
I have a wife and four pink boys. I spin
on all this stupid metaphysic now
because last afternoon we visited
some friends in town. After the pecan pie,
I drank until my forehead smacked the table,
and woke to find my shirt crusted with blood.
When Mary didn't yell at me, I knew
she finally understood that I was gone,
dissolving back. As we rode home, I tried
to say, *I'm sorry, Hon.* The carriage bucked
across the mud-dried ruts and I shut up.
And she, in August heat, just sat, head cocked
as if for chills hidden in the hot, damp breeze,
as if they were a sound, time merely distance.
O Death, I know exactly where it is —
your sting. And, Grave, I know your victory.

That night, around the tents, the boys caught fireflies,
pinched them in half, and smeared them on their nails,
then ran through pine-dark woods, waving their hands.
All I could hear was laughter, shouts. And all
that I could see for each one of my sons
were ten blurs of faint, artificial light,
never too far apart, and trembling.
Like fairies, magic, sprites, they ran and shouted,
"I'm not real! I'm not real!" The whole world fell
away from me — perhaps I was still drunk —
as on the night Titania told dazed Bottom,
"Put off your human grossness so, and like
an airy spirit go." But even then
the night could not hold long against the light,
and light destroys roots, fog, lies, orchids, night,
dawn stars, the moon, delusions, and most magic.
And light sends into hiding owls, fireflies,
and bats, whom for their unerring blunder, I
adore the most of all night fliers. But owls,
hid in a hickory, will hoot all day,
and even the moon persists, like my hangover,
some days till almost noon, drifting above
the harsh, bright, murderous morning light — so blue,
so valuable, so much like currency
that if the moon were my blue coin, I'd never spend it.

THE HOLE IN THE TENT

The chemical smell of skunk drifts past my tent.
There's one thing you can say about a skunk:
it actually smells better as it rots.
And this one here is very much alive.
The smell floats through a hole that started out
a frayed spot in the thin, confederate canvas.
At night, the whole tent — closed and close — swells taut
with breathing. It's like living inside
my own blast-furnace lungs. So one night, fretful,
I jabbed my walking stick through the worn cloth
and, twisting on my side, I saw the three
stars of Orion's belt, but not the sword
that hangs from it and not the pinprick stars
of hands, feet, head — just three stars in a line
that's almost straight, and I felt, if I reached
out with my walking stick, I could, almost,
tap straight the misplaced star.

During the day,
I sit here with a rusty barlow knife
and carve, as best I can, a rattler's head
onto my stick. It too is almost straight,
a limb of hickory that I lean on
whenever I, as bent as Moses, try
to walk. Well, hobble really. When Mary's gone
I tear the small hole more so it can vent
the heat that radiates from me. And Mary
sleeps with the boys and lets me thrash.
She says she could fry bacon on my head.
The poets say that love is like a fever:
you burn with it, you thrash, and cannot sleep.
I say my fever's the most passionate,

fierce lover I have known. She's always here
to warm my feet. But then she turns as cold
as a snowdrift. She's jealous of my wife.
She works to keep the two of us apart.
Ours is a greedy, pagan love — intense
and crippling as any mad amour.
But when I die, this bitch will die with me.

Or maybe not. The ancients thought the soul,
at death, slips from the death-slack mouth, escapes,
and makes a cosmic beeline straight to God.
That's always sounded accurate to me.
Outside my flesh, it will dart through the hole
I've made for it — hole in the whole, rent in the tent,
a bolt hole for my fever and my soul,
in case they're not the same, though often I
suspect they are. As rabbits from a fox
will bolt into the ground, my soul will bolt
into the air. Escape. Escape. Escape.
But I admire also the stubborn skunk,
who stands his ground and stinks the whole place up.
We keep some chickens near our campground. They
enliven things with cackles, fussing, food.
And when — loud squawks at night! — one disappears,
I just assume it is Br'er Skunk, Br'er Possum,
or even my old friend the fox, whom I
do not begrudge a hen occasionally.
Our chickens also fascinate the hawks.
In bed and staring out the hole, I've watched
hawks circle high above our hot tents, watching
the panicked hens. And every now and then

a hawk swoops down and I, hoping to see
its God-like predatory strike, throw back
the tent flap, scaring off the fierce impact
I yearn to see. But from one red-tailed hawk
a dollop of scat dropped free and fell somewhere
out far across the vast expanse of pine,
and for a moment — a long moment — I,
since I would never touch the bird itself,
longed to go find its drop of scat.

But that

is not the thing I think of most these days.
This is: Two skunks are caught in one steel trap.
I'm going to chew my foot off and escape,
one says. Next day, he hobbles past and finds
his friend still caught. *What're you waiting for?*
he asks. *The trapper will be back here soon.*
Annoyed, the other skunk replies, *I know.*
But what more can I do? I've already chewed
two of my feet off and I'm not free yet.

THE HOUSE OF THE LORD FOREVER

Where will you spend eternity?
he asked. He'd marched out of the woods
into our clearing, paused, then made
a beeline right to me. A vine
of ivy clung to his boot heel and dragged
behind him in the dirt. His black
suit coat was soaked clean through with sweat.
He hunkered down beside my head
and asked again, *Where will you spend*
eternity? I craned my neck around
to look him in the face. His worn
cavalry pants were stuffed into his boots.
From my position, lying on my back,
I got a good close look at them:
cracked, half-soled, reheeled riding boots,
once black, now gray with age. I'd wager
he rode with Mosby, Quantrill — one
of those bastards: it would have made
a preacher out of me. *Where will*
you spend eternity?
"With God."
And where is God? he quizzed.
"Oh dear,"
I said. "Don't tell me you've misplaced Him."

He sputtered, stood up — shocked. I used
the time to pull myself erect
and, leaning on my walking stick,
smooth out my clothes. He tried again.
Where's God?
"Which God is that? The God

who wiped out Sodom and Gomorrah?
The God who punished Saul because
he spared a few Amelekites
and let some oxen live? That God
seems like a military man — a Mosby
or Quantrill. At midnight, He rides down,
arrests the federal train, and cuts
the foreskins off a thousand Philistines."
Enraged, shouting, I paused for breath,
and Mary, who'd walked over, frowned
and walked back to the fire. He blanched.

I think, sir, you are being flip
with me. Be calm. Don't you desire
to dwell in the house of the Lord forever?

"And what," I asked, "is this?" — palms spread
to indicate the camp. Just then,
at that chance moment, Mary dumped
the morning coffee on the coals.
They sputtered, sizzled, sighed. The rich
scent rose around the three of us,
like perfume, like flames rising around
three men cast in the fiery furnace.
But was the fourth man here or not?
My jack-leg preacher flailed his hands.
Don't you trust in the world beyond
these shadows?

"Well, Preacher," I said,
"you've heard about the blind skunk that
fell in love with a fart?"

May God
have mercy on your soul! His tone
implied the Deity would not,
in fact, be so remiss. He stalked
into the woods. The vine of ivy trailed
behind him like a snake he'd crushed,
or almost crushed, beneath his heel.
Perhaps I'm simply being cruel
with metaphor. I can't decide.
But Mary glowered disapprovingly
at me, as if I'd done a meanness,
killed someone's goddamn albatross
or something. And maybe — sure —
I had. But I don't care. I won't
debate my soul with strangers — not
when I have family who pray
for me so urgently I swear
their fierce prayers surface in my dreams
like the underground wrenching of wings,
brown wings, that form, beat slowly, dig
toward air, toward me, as if they would
lunge on my back and fasten, beat,
flail, lift, and carry me aloft.
But I imagine differently:
not butterfly or angel wings,
not swan or nightingale or heron —
instead the dark brown random wings
of bats, of moths. Or none.
How can
they be so sure? They are so sure.

LOVE LETTER FROM THE GRAVE, BURNT

I'm out of this. But you're still scoured by
each grief, each savagery the lock-step heart
is subject to. There is a balm
in Gilead, but you must carry on,
burning, acquiring the need for Gilead,

the legendary balm that soothes the soul.
Forgive my teasing. Although the body has
no elegance, it has the facts.
I can dissuade it for a little while
but it will end the argument. And soon.

Ten days at most. This letter is unfair.
Before you read it you'll have stood, a widow,
above the northeast corner of my face.
You may have wept. Or, maybe, for the boys,
you were dry-eyed, much braver than the day

required of you. What makes me speculate
about these damn unknowables? You said *goodbye,*
thinking that graveside word would end
our love, our commerce. Now I'm here with this —

a letter from the grave, confused enough
to be the whole man coming back to claim
the thin authority of a revenant.
I know it isn't fair or kind. I know
it has a false poignancy no matter what

I say. Or fail to say. I know all this.
But I will tell you something stupid, Mary.

We dead don't get around much anymore.
We have no self-control. We are concerned with nothing
but ourselves. The Bible says there is a time

to refrain from embracing. We're almost there.
Forgive me, Love. Though it may scrub
your red grief raw, I can't resist the chance
to come back just this once — this final time —
and kiss you when you least expect a kiss.

DYING

The pistol underneath my head
is cold. On August nights, it seems
the only cold thing in the world.
Life's dangerous out here, in woods,
and I don't even have the lungs
to play my flute. No tune I know
is simple, slow, and tremulous enough
to fit my breath. Which means, of course,
the pistol is a waste of time.
I'm not sure I could lift the stupid thing.
But I'm content to feel the iron
beneath my pillow: protector of the hearth,
defender of Confederate womanhood,
et cetera — a role I play
for Mary, who loves me, who'll grieve,
who loved me back before I knew
the heart — a hammer, anvil, forge —
could hold our flaws, and burn and beat them
into something useful: from sin
to virtue, battlefield to garden,
and suffering to grace, somehow.
Well, anyway, that's my best theory.

When we still lived, up to our necks
in debt, on Denmead Street, I'd loll
back in the tub and read the paper.
The water cooled. I'd holler, *"Mary!"*
She'd lug in boiling water, dump
it in the tub, go boil some more,
as if I could deserve such care.
What did I do for her? I made her laugh.

We had a fat tomcat who loved her
as if she were his god. He watched
her as she slept, left headless squirrels
and sparrows by the door; and when
she swept, he stalked the dust balls, pounced,
so Mary could admire his skills.
The afternoon that we conceived
our youngest — Rob — we rose from sex
and found the goddamn cat had sprayed my socks.
He cowered underneath the bed,
while I, down on my hands and knees,
swatted at him with my wet socks,
till Mary kicked my lifted rear.
My head smacked the bed frame. The cat
raced off and Mary laughed. Me too.
Two years. My lungs have been so weak
we last made love two years ago.

I think of this because this afternoon
she tilted my head back into her lap
and spread my hair across the blue
cloth of her dress. Slowly, with Job's
long patience, she combed through my head,
picking through each dark, separate strand,
finding the lice and crushing them,
one by one, beneath her fingernail.
Such life that clings to me! Such death
it takes to keep my body clean!
This is the greatest gift: to know
that someone sees you as you are
and loves you anyway. She must

have seen them when, last night, she slipped
into my dark tent and pulled off
her sweater. Sparks crackled, flew. In bed,
she pressed that fierce, electric body
— more full of light than it could hold —
against my flesh. And it responded.
My Lord, I didn't think it could.
She hiked her dress and mounted me.
I never saw her body, just felt
the moist engulfing of my flesh,
the holding deep inside, unmoving: me,
unable to move; her, still, choosing not to,
a long time. Sobs broke from her mouth,
sweat soaked her dark blue dress, and she
rode me as I would ride a horse I loved,
knowing the orders that I carried
were more important than the horse,
and knowing, too, it didn't matter
whether the flailed horse lived. She fell,
exhausted, on my face. Too weak
to push her off, I breathed her rich
sweat smell and tasted its faint salt.
She pressed her lips against my ear
and said, "I'm sorry." I said it back.
The words were not exactly right
but we both needed to forgive
our lives — and be forgiven. We'd touched
the big death with the little one,
the way, on entering a woman,
a sentimental man might pause
a long time, simply being there,

inside, knowing he'll soon begin
to move, withdraw, re-enter her
until he comes. But he might first
hold still as long as possible
before — at last, inevitably —
he starts to move, knowing that first
loves last, caresses it, and enters
and enters it again, till, awed,
they merge in elegiac shuddering.

But since I, breathless, couldn't move, she moved.

THE HEREAFTER

Some people as they die grow fierce, afraid.
They see a bright light, offer frantic prayers,
and try to climb them, like Jacob's ladder, up
to heaven. Others, never wavering,
inhabit heaven years before they die,
so certain of their grace they can describe,
down to the gingerbread around the eaves,
the cottage God has saved for them. For hours
they'll talk of how the willow will not weep,
the flowering Judas not betray. They'll talk
of how they'll finally learn to play the flute
and speak good French.

Still others know they'll rot
and their flesh turn to earth, which will become
live oaks, spreading their leaves in August light.
The green cathedral glow that shines through them
will light grandchildren playing hide-and-seek
inside the grove. My next-door neighbor says
he's glad the buzzards will at last give wings
to those of us who've envied swifts as they
swoop, twist, and race through tight mosquito runs.

And some — my brother's one — anticipate
the grave as if it were a chair pulled up
before a fire on winter nights. His ghost,
he thinks, will slouch into the velvet cushion,
a bourbon and branchwater in its hand.
I've even met a man who says the soul
will come back in another skin — the way
a renter moves from house to house. Myself,
I'd like to come back as my father's hound.
Or something fast: a deer, a rust-red fox.

For so long I have thought of us as nails
God drives into the oak floor of this world,
it's hard to comprehend the hammer turned
to claw me out. I'm joking, mostly. I love
the possibilities — not one or two
but all of them. So if I had to choose,
pick only one and let the others go,
my death would be less strange, less rich, less like
a dizzying swig of fine rotgut. I roll
the busthead, slow, across my tongue and taste
the copper coils, the mockingbird that died
from fumes and plunged, wings spread, into the mash.
And underneath it all, just barely there,
I find the scorched-nut hint of corn that grew
in fields I walked, flourished beneath a sun
that warmed my skin, swaying in a changing wind
that tousled, stung, caressed, and toppled me.

ACKNOWLEDGMENTS

Grateful acknowledgment is made to the following magazines in which some of the poems here were first published: *The Chicago Review:* "Memories of Lookout Prison." *Crazyhorse:* "Glyphs." *The Hudson Review:* "The Hereafter," "He Imagines His Wife Dead," "His Wife," "The Yellow Steeple." *The Missouri Review:* "Appetite for Poison," "Serenades in Virginia: Summer 1863," "What the Light Destroys," "Sufficient Witness," "A Husband on the Marsh." *MSS:* "The Cult of the Lost Cause," "Fever," "Fishkill on the Chattahoochee," "In San Antonio," "Postcards of the Hanging," "A Rapprochement with Death," "Raven Days," "Reflections on Cold Harbor," "The World of Turtles: On the Georgia Coast." *The Nation:* "Child on the Marsh." *The New England Review:* "Dying," "The House of the Lord Forever." *The Ontario Review:* "First Anniversary." *Ploughshares:* "After the Wilderness: May 3, 1863," "A Christian on the Marsh." *The Reaper:* "War's End." *The Seattle Review:* "At the Kymulga Grist Mill." *Sequoia:* "The House on Denmead Street." *Shankpainter:* "Flauto Primo." *The Southern Review:* "After the Lost War," "Around the Campfire," "At Chancellorsville: The Battle of the Wilderness," "Burial Detail," "A Father on the Marsh," "The Last Time I Saw General Lee: An Idyll," "Listen! The Flies," "Love Letter from the Grave, Burnt," "On the Killing Floor," "A Soldier on the Marsh," "The Summer of the Drought."

"After the Lost War" is reprinted from *Saints and Strangers* (Boston: Houghton Mifflin, 1985). "Postcards of the Hanging" was reprinted in *Pushcart Prizes, VII: Best of the Small Presses* (Wainscott,

N.Y.: Pushcart Press, 1983). "His Wife" and "The Yellow Steeple" were reprinted in the *Anthology of Magazine Verse and Yearbook of American Poetry* (Beverly Hills, Calif.: Monitor Books, 1984).

For my purposes, the most useful biographies of Sidney Lanier were Edwin Mims's *Sidney Lanier* (Boston: Houghton Mifflin, 1905) and Aubrey Harrison Starke's *Sidney Lanier* (Chapel Hill, N.C.: University of North Carolina Press, 1933). The latter is such a thorough book that it has obviated, for more than fifty years, the need for a successor. For Lanier's work itself, there is the Centennial Edition of the *Complete Works*. In 1983, when I was a little less than halfway through this book, Ed Folsom of the University of Iowa gave me a complete set of the Centennial Edition, and I would like to thank him again for his generosity.

"Love Letter from the Grave" is dedicated to Eric Pankey and Jennifer Atkinson. I owe a special debt of gratitude to Liz Rosenberg for her early and continued encouragement of this book.

For residencies and for fellowships that made possible the writing of this book, I would like to thank Yaddo, the MacDowell Colony, the Fine Arts Work Center at Provincetown, the National Endowment for the Arts, and the Ingram Merrill Foundation.